HOT TO TROT

AN AGATHA RAISIN MYSTERY

HOT TO TROT

M. C. BEATON
with R. W. Green

THORNDIKE PRESS
A part of Gale, a Cengage Company

GALE
A Cengage Company

Thorndike Press® Large Print Mystery.
The text of this Large Print edition is unabridged.
Other aspects of the book may vary from the original edition.
Set in 16 pt. Plantin.

**LIBRARY OF CONGRESS CIP DATA ON FILE.
CATALOGUING IN PUBLICATION FOR THIS BOOK
IS AVAILABLE FROM THE LIBRARY OF CONGRESS.**

ISBN-13: 978-1-4328-8427-7 (hardcover alk. paper)

Published in 2021 by arrangement with St. Martin's Publishing

Printed in Mexico
Print Number: 01   Print Year: 2021

For M. C. Beaton, with love —
her warmth, intelligence and sense of
humour will be missed by her readers,
but even more so by her friends
and family. The world will be a
less interesting place without her.

FOREWORD BY R. W. GREEN

He simply had to be up to something — or *she* was. It was all a bit fishy, or so Agatha Raisin would have thought. A married man calling on a woman of advancing years and spending hours having cosy little private chats? Agatha would have thought there was definitely something going on . . . and there was. M. C. Beaton — Marion — was working out what agonies and triumphs would next befall Agatha Raisin, and her male visitor — me — had the immense thrill and huge privilege of helping her do it.

I first met Marion many years ago. My wife, Krystyna, was Marion's publisher in London for more than twenty years, so Marion and I met many times at publishing functions. We enjoyed chatting, both being Scots, both having been journalists, and both being writers. Marion, it has to be said, was a far more successful journalist and writer than me, but she was always as keen to find out what I was up to as I was to hear stories about her adventures in Scotland, the United States, France or the Mediterranean. She had led a fascinating life.

At publishing events, Marion was inevitably whisked away to meet and greet, but when Krystyna and I visited her in the Cotswolds on occasion, we were able to talk more freely, sometimes about books, more often not. I came to regard Marion as a friend and always looked forward to seeing her. Last year, when she was not in good health and finding it difficult to get her ideas down on paper, I was glad to be able to help.

Marion was an avid news watcher, following world events on TV, and they were a bountiful source of inspiration for her. Current affairs stories regularly reminded her of events from her own past, which she would sometimes mould into scenes involving Agatha, James, Charles or the village of Carsely. Those scenes might suggest plots, or a way to develop a storyline. The scenes she planned stayed in her head until they were committed to paper as part of a plot device or something to add to the life story of one of her large cast of regular characters. She knew everything about her characters. She knew where they lived, how they talked, how they dressed, how they moved and what they thought. She didn't regard them as friends — they were her inventions, not her closest chums — but she knew them all intimately nonetheless. And she kept all of their character traits and quirky foibles in her head. She had no need of any kind of character bible or written notes.

Sir Charles Fraith, for example, was described to me by Marion as "a predator when it comes to women." She was quick to point out that she didn't mean he is dangerous or violent towards women, simply that he always has one eye on his next conquest. He is well-bred, well-educated and intelligent but, despite his grand house and vast estate, he is, as she put it, "impecunious." That, she swiftly explained, was not the sort of word she liked to use very often in her books. Marion liked to keep her stories moving along briskly, having fun, travelling light, unencumbered by excessively ornate prose.

When I visited Marion to start working with her, I expected that she might want me to take dictation on the new book and possibly chip in a few ideas as we went along. No. She was smarter than that. She wanted to talk about storylines, incidents, murders and what cards the characters would be dealt. Marion did not, for example, want Sir Charles Fraith to remain penniless forever. She thought it would be good for him to have lots of money for a change. How long she would allow him to keep it was another matter.

I made lots of notes, all the while expecting a dictation session to begin. That wasn't Marion's idea at all. She wanted to make sure that I understood Agatha's world, so she sent me away with my notes to write a sample chapter the way she would do it, staying true to the characters and the way that life, death and murder played out in Carsely. If what I came up with was the way she would weave an Agatha Raisin murder investigation, then we might be able to work together. If it wasn't as she wanted, well, we would still be friends.

It's easy to forget how horribly nervous you used to feel as a child in the classroom, handing a homework essay to the teacher. It all came flooding back when I gave Marion the print-out of what I had written. I wasn't exactly hopping from one foot to the other as Marion read through it — I sat down to avoid that — but the silence was excruciating. Suddenly, without looking up, she said, "No, I wouldn't use that phrase," and crossed out a line with her pen. A moment later, "Not 'smirk.' Agatha doesn't 'smirk.'"

Then she looked up and smiled. "Apart from that, this is just how I'd have done it."

Agatha would not only have been deeply suspicious of our clandestine meetings, but also absolutely furious about the laughs we had at her expense. A phrase involving snakes springs to mind. Marion and I were of one mind in having fun with the writing — otherwise, how could it ever be fun to read? I thoroughly enjoyed working with Marion and I am honoured that she trusted me to meddle with her characters. I will miss her more than I can say.

AN INTRODUCTION FROM M. C. BEATON ON THE AGATHA RAISIN SERIES

The writing road leading to Agatha Raisin is a long one.

When I left school, I became a fiction buyer for John Smith & Son Ltd. on St. Vincent Street, Glasgow, the oldest bookshop in Britain — alas, now closed. Those were the days when bookselling was a profession and one had to know something about every book in the shop.

I developed an eye for what sort of book a customer might want, and could, for example, spot an arriving request for a leatherbound pocket-sized edition of Omar Khayyam at a hundred paces.

As staff were allowed to borrow books, I was able to feed my addiction for detective and spy stories. As a child, my first love had been Richard Hannay in John Buchan's *The Thirty-Nine Steps*. Then, on my eleventh birthday, I was given a copy of Dorothy L. Sayers's *Lord Peter Views the Body* and read everything by that author I could get. After that came, courtesy of the bookshop, Ngaio Marsh, Josephine Tey, Gladys Mitchell, Eric Ambler, Agatha Christie and very many more.

Bookselling was a very genteel job. We were not allowed to call each other by our first names. I was given half an hour in the morning to go out for coffee, an hour and a half for lunch, and half an hour in the afternoon for tea.

I was having coffee one morning when I was joined by a customer, Mary Kavanagh, who recognised me. She said she was features editor of the Glasgow edition of the *Daily Mail* and wanted a reporter to cover a production of *Cinderella* at the Rutherglen Rep that evening, because the editor's nephew was acting as one of the Ugly Sisters, but all the reporters refused to go.

"I'll go," I said eagerly.

She looked at me doubtfully. "Have you had anything published?"

"Oh, yes," I said, lying through my teeth. "*Punch, The Listener,* things like that."

"Well, it's only fifty words," she said. "All right."

And that was the start. I rose up through vaudeville and then became lead theatre critic at the age of nineteen.

After that, I became fashion editor of *Scottish Field* magazine and then moved to the *Scottish Daily Express* as Scotland's new emergent writer and proceeded to submerge. The news editor gave me a tryout to save me from being sacked, and I became a crime reporter.

People often ask if this experience was to help me in the future with writing detective stories. Yes, but not in the way they think. The crime in Glasgow was awful: razor gangs, axmen, reporting stories in filthy gaslit tenements where the stair lavatory had broken, and so, as an escape, I kept making up stories in my head that had nothing to do with reality. Finally, it all became too much for me and I got a transfer to the *Daily Express* on Fleet Street, London.

I enjoyed being a Fleet Street reporter. I would walk down Fleet Street in the evening if I was on the late shift and feel the thud of the printing presses and smell the aroma of hot paper and see St. Paul's, floodlit, floating above Ludgate Hill, and felt I had truly arrived.

I became chief woman reporter just as boredom and reality were setting in. That was when I met my husband, Harry Scott Gibbons, former Middle East correspondent for the paper who had just resigned to write a book, *The Conspirators,* about the British withdrawal from Aden.

I resigned as well and we went on our travels, through Greece, Turkey and Cyprus. Harry was now engaged in writing a book about the Cyprus troubles. We arrived back in London, broke, and I had a baby, Charles. We moved to America when Harry found work as an editor at the *Oyster Bay Guardian,* a Long Island newspaper. That was not a very pleasant experience.

But I longed to write fiction. I had read all of Georgette Heyer's Regency romances and thought I would try some of the new ones that were coming out. I complained to my husband, "They're awful. The history's wrong, the speech is wrong, and the dress is wrong."

"Well, write one," he urged.

My mother had been a great fan of the Regency period and I had been brought up on Jane Austen and various history books. She even found out-of-print books from the period, such as Maria Edgeworth's *Moral Tales.* I remember with affection a villain called Lord Raspberry. So I cranked up the film in my head and began to write what was there. The first book was called *Regency Gold.* I had only done about twenty pages, blocked by the thought that surely I couldn't really write a whole book, when my husband took them from me and showed them to a writer friend who recommended an agent. So I went on and wrote the first fifty pages and plot and sent it all to the agent Barbara Lowenstein. She suggested some changes, and after making them I took the lot back to her.

The book sold in three days flat. Then, before it was even finished, I got an offer from another publisher to write Edwardian romances, which I did under the name of Jennie Tremaine because my maiden name, Marion Chesney, was contracted to the first publisher. Other publishers followed, other names: Ann Fairfax, Helen Crampton and Charlotte Ward.

I was finally contracted by St. Martin's Press to write six hardback Regency series at a time. But I wanted to write mysteries, and discussed my ambition to do so with my editor at St. Martin's Press, Hope Dellon. "Okay," she said. "Who's your detective?"

I had only got as far as the rough idea and hadn't thought of one. "The village bobby," I said hurriedly.

"What's his name?"

I quickly racked my brains. "Hamish Macbeth."

I had to find not only a name for my detective but a new name for myself. "Give me a name that isn't Mac something," suggested Hope. She said that M. C. Beaton would be a good name, keeping the M. C. for Marion Chesney.

So I began to write detective stories. We moved back to London to further our son's education and it was there that the idea for the first Agatha Raisin was germinated, though I did not know it at the time.

My son's housemaster asked me if I could do some home baking for a charity sale. I did not want to let my son down by telling him I couldn't bake. So I went to Waitrose and bought two quiches, carefully removed the shop wrappings, put my own wrappings on with a homemade label, and delivered them. They were a great success.

Shortly afterwards, Hope, who is very fond of the Cotswolds, asked me if I would consider writing a detective story set in that scenic area. I wanted the detective to be a woman. I had enjoyed E. F. Benson's Miss Mapp books and thought it might be interesting to create a detective that the reader might not like but nonetheless would want to win in the end. I was also inspired by the amusing detective stories of Colin Watson in his Flaxborough novels and Simon Brett's detective, Charles Paris.

Agatha Raisin will continue to live in the Cotswolds because the very placid beauty of the place, with its winding lanes and old cottages, serves as a constant to the often abrasive Agatha. I am only sorry that I continue to inflict so much murder and mayhem on this tranquil setting.

CHAPTER ONE

No one knew. No one who encountered Agatha Raisin striding purposefully along Mircester High Street on this gloriously sunny spring morning, her brown hair sleek and lustrous in its neat bob courtesy of a pre-breakfast appointment with her hairdresser, could possibly have known. No one could even have suspected that the woman in the elegantly cut navy-blue jacket and skirt, carrying a dusky-pink shoulder bag that very nearly matched the colour of her lipstick, who was smiling and nodding pleasantly to passers-by, was hiding a dark torment.

Only Agatha knew how bitter and betrayed she felt about the way her long-time friend and sometime lover, Sir Charles Fraith, had committed to marrying a woman almost thirty years younger than her. Only Agatha knew, and that, she had decided, was how it was going to stay. I am a successful, independent woman, she told herself. I don't need to lumber myself with regret over Charles's mistakes. I need to get on with my own life. Wasn't it Coco Chanel who said, "A girl should be two things — who and what she wants"? Well, that and the little black dress were two things she definitely got right. I am a private investigator with a thriving business to run and I will live my life the way I choose. Anyone who doesn't agree with that can go to hell — and that includes Sir Charles Fraith! At that precise moment, Agatha almost believed herself.

Reaching the corner of an ancient cobbled lane that tumbled away from the high street down a shallow slope, Agatha looked up to the first-floor windows of Raisin Investigations. She could see her staff milling around, preparing themselves for the working day. She tiptoed, as elegantly as she could manage, the three or four steps it took to cross the cobbles, avoiding embedding the high heels of her dark-blue suede shoes in the evil cracks between the stones that she knew were lurking there, booby traps for the unwary. Reaching the sanctuary of the pavement outside the antiques shop above which were her offices, she caught her reflection in the shop window. A little stocky, perhaps, she admitted to herself, but what could you expect after a long, cold winter eating hearty meals? She would easily lose a few pounds now that salad season was approaching. She tugged at the hem of her jacket to straighten an imagined bulge, gave herself a nod of approval and made her way upstairs.

"Morning, all!" she announced, bustling into the office.

Everyone looked towards her and responded. Toni Gilmour, Agatha's Girl Friday, was young, beautiful, blonde and a meticulous detective with a good eye for detail. Agatha had come to rely on her a great deal, although that was something she seldom admitted to anyone, especially Toni. Patrick Mulligan was a tall, cadaverous retired policeman with a wealth of experience as an investigator. He had a serious, almost sombre demeanour and seldom smiled. Simon Black, on the other hand, greeted Agatha with a wide grin that wrinkled his features. He had an odd, pale, angular face that Agatha could never describe as handsome, yet he was a young man who was never short of attractive girls hanging on his arm or warming his bed — or so he claimed. The only girl he ever seemed to care about, however, was the next one. As an investigator, he had his shortcomings, but his casual charm and dogged determination usually saw him through.

Mrs. Freedman, Agatha's secretary, who handled most of the company admin, stepped forward to offer her a blue plastic document wallet. A middle-aged woman with a kindly expression, Helen Freedman was hard-working and efficient, and appeared to know by instinct precisely when Agatha wanted either a cup of coffee in the morning, a cup of tea in the afternoon, or a gin and tonic whenever.

"Some invoices for you to approve," she said, "a couple of letters to sign, and can I remind you that you need to submit your expenses?"

"Thank you, Helen," said Agatha. "I'll sort that out later today. All right, everyone! Case conference catch-up in my office in ten minutes."

She crossed the open area to her own separate office, pushing open the door. The small room was dominated by a huge wooden desk that had aspirations to being Georgian but, sadly, had been made three hundred years too late. She dropped the blue wallet on the desk beside her large cut-glass ashtray. It had been several months since she had last smoked a cigarette and at one time she had banished all ashtrays to drawers and cupboards, keeping the smoking accoutrements out of sight and out of mind. This one, however, she retained as a kind of trophy, now used only as a paperweight, the glass sparkling clean, a reminder of her triumph over tobacco.

Settling into her chair, she took a copy of the local newspaper from her bag and unfolded it. "Society Wedding of the Year," announced the headline. "Sir Charles Fraith to marry in lavish ceremony at Barfield House." Agatha sighed. So much fuss. Charles's vile fiancée, Mary Darlinda Brown-Field, was making sure that her wedding was being splashed across the pages of every rag whose editor she could charm, coax, buy or bully. The article was accompanied by a photograph of them together. Charles had a vague, haunted expression, while Mary — well, the giant chin she had inherited from her father and the eyes that were set just a little too far apart meant that she would never win the Mircester Maids beauty contest. Yet the way she was holding on to Charles's arm demonstrated her determination to make this the biggest wedding ever covered by the *Mircester Telegraph.*

It wasn't even as if Charles hadn't previously had a lavish ceremony at Barfield

House. Agatha had scuppered that one by turning up with the Spanish waiter who was the rightful father of the pregnant bride's unborn child. This time, however, there seemed no way of stopping Charles from plunging himself into a life of misery. This was a marriage of convenience, a financial transaction that he saw as a way of propping up his ailing estate. Yet the bride's family's money could never buy them that which they craved — the social status denied them by their lowly pedigree. The marriage was a sham, and Agatha worried that Charles risked losing control of the house and estate that had been in his family for generations. Yet she had made little effort to extricate him from this latest predicament, and now there was no time. The wedding was on Saturday — only forty-eight hours away.

Her staff filed into her office carrying cups of coffee and dragging chairs close to her desk. Mrs. Freedman provided Agatha with a coffee, then returned to the outer office.

Toni sat closest to Agatha. She glanced at the newspaper lying on the desk and reached out to turn it towards her in order to read the smaller print. Agatha placed the blue document wallet on top of it and Toni looked up to see her boss staring impassively at her. She glanced away and sipped her coffee. Clearly the wedding was not a topic for open discussion.

"Right," said Agatha. "Let's start with the Chadwick divorce case. You've been keeping tabs on Mrs. Sheraton Chadwick, Simon. What sort of woman are we dealing with?"

"She has the look of someone who likes a bit of rumpy-pumpy, if you know what I mean," said Simon, grinning and cocking an eyebrow.

"I'm not sure that I do know what you mean," said Agatha innocently. "Have you any ideas, Toni?"

"Rumpy-pumpy? I can't be certain," said Toni, taking her cue from Agatha and adopting a naïvely perplexed expression, "but it sounds like one of those phrases they used in old British black-and-white movies."

"Ah, yes," Agatha agreed. "Like 'slap and tickle' or 'hanky-panky.' Simon, do you mean that she seemed to you like the sort of woman who might enjoy an enthusiastic illicit sex life?"

"Yes," said Simon, squirming slightly. Patrick Mulligan raised a hand to his mouth to cover one of his rare smiles. "Yes, that's what I mean."

Agatha placed the palms of her hands on her desk and leaned forward slightly, fixing Simon with her dark bear-like eyes. "Let's keep the language we use at meetings a bit more formal, shall we? If we get sloppy when discussing cases, there's every chance one of us might slip up when talking to a client and say something out of turn. We can't have people thinking that we treat our work like some kind of joke. That would definitely be bad for business."

"Sorry," Simon apologised, sitting up straight, a slight flush colouring his cheeks. "I will watch how I . . . um . . . phrase things in the future."

"Good," said Agatha. "How has the surveillance been going?"

"I haven't had much luck yet. Mrs. Chadwick has been visited by a bloke at a rented house in Oxford."

"And do you have photographs of this . . . bloke?"

"I've seen him, but I could never get a shot of his face that could be used to identify him," Simon admitted. "I did get the number of the car that dropped him off and picked him up, but he's out of the vehicle and into the house like a flash."

"Okay, let's move on," said Agatha. "Patrick, where are we with the Philpott Electronics case?"

"The company chairman, Sidney Philpott, has concerns about his new managing director, Harold Cheeseman," said Patrick, sliding a manila folder across the desk. "He has asked us to carry out a discreet background check. So far Cheeseman's CV and references all appear to be genuine. He left his last job to take up a post in Australia, but told Mr. Philpott that he came back because Australia was not to his wife's liking. He's definitely lying about that."

"What makes you say that?" Agatha asked, flicking through the report.

"His wife is dead," Patrick explained. "She died long before he left for Australia. That was one of his reasons for going — to make a fresh start."

"It's a weird thing to lie about," said Agatha.

"He may have his reasons," Patrick conceded, "but I'm not at all sure about him. From the way the staff say he has been acting at work, there's something odd going on. I've sent a couple of emails to Australia to find out what he got up to there, and I'm tracking down some of his old friends here."

"Okay," said Agatha. "Stay on it."

There was a handful of other ongoing cases to discuss, mainly divorces and missing pets, before Agatha turned to Toni.

"So, Toni," she said. "Any potential new cases that I haven't yet heard about?"

"We have been contacted by a Mr. Gutteridge, who runs a biscuit and cake factory near Evesham," said Toni. "He wants us to install listening devices in the workers' canteen because he thinks the staff are saying nasty things about him and his secretary."

"Are they having an affair? What sort of things does he think they're saying?"

"He denies any affair. She comes from Geneva, and graffiti in the ladies' loo calls her his 'Swiss roll.' "

"I don't want to get involved in that," said Agatha, shaking her head. "I don't mind us sweeping a place to remove bugs, but I won't plant them in order to eavesdrop on ordinary people simply to deal with office gossip. Anything else?"

"We have a Mrs. Jessop, who believes that a poltergeist is rearranging her kitchen cupboards and digging up her garden."

"A poltergeist?" said Agatha. "A ghost? Creepy, but interesting."

"And," said Toni, "Mrs. Fletcher, who lives just outside Carsely, wants us to investigate someone dumping at the bottom of her garden."

"Dumping?" said Patrick. "You mean fly-tipping? Leaving piles of rubbish? That's a matter for the local council, isn't it?"

"No, not fly-tipping," said Toni. "Someone has been having a dump. Leaving piles of excrement. Quite a lot of it, she says."

"That's disgusting," said Agatha, wrinkling her nose. "Who would do a thing like that?"

"She has no idea," Toni explained, "but the piles are being added to on a regular basis in the middle of the night."

"Right," said Agatha, drawing the meeting to a close. "Let's keep everything moving forward. Patrick, can you use your contacts to try to trace the car that dropped off Mrs. Chadwick's visitor? Toni and I will take over the Chadwick case to see if we can make some progress there. We will also find out if Mrs. Jessop's poltergeist is worth investigating. Simon, you can take on the case of the phantom pooper."

"But that's . . ." Simon's objection wilted under the weight of Agatha's withering stare.

"Yes, I know — it's a shit job," she said, "but somebody has to do it, and the quicker you clear it up, the sooner you can move on to something else."

Simon and Patrick dragged their chairs away, heading for the door, but Agatha motioned Toni to stay.

"I need you to get up to speed on the Chadwick case," she said. "Give me a call later and we can meet up to stake out that house tonight. I will be out of the office this afternoon."

"Are you going to see Charles?"

"That's none of your business."

"You really have to try to talk to him . . ."

"I don't *have* to do anything of the sort!" Agatha scowled, a note of anger in her voice.

"You need to do something," said Toni. "This has been plaguing you for months. You had a thoroughly miserable Christmas and you've been on edge ever since. You need to come to terms with what's happening."

"I am perfectly capable of deciding what I will or will not do, and I certainly do *not* need personal advice from someone as young as you — someone who was still in nappies when I was being wined and dined by some of London's most eligible bachelors!"

"And how did that work out?" said Toni, struggling to subdue her own rising temper. "You ended up abandoning London to live in the Cotswolds. Look, we've been through a lot together and I care about —"

"I don't need you to care about anything

except your work!" barked Agatha. "I shouldn't have to explain —"

"Well I'm *so* sorry!" Toni snapped. "It must be very difficult explaining *anything* to someone as young as me!"

"Not at all," said Agatha, "but I left the crayons and colouring books at home to-day."

Toni stormed out and Agatha snatched the newspaper from the desk, hurling it into the waste-paper basket. She knew that Toni was trying to help, motivated by the best of intentions, but the situation with Charles had been festering for so long that the slightest mention of it plunged her into a cauldron of fury. With a sigh, she reluctantly admitted to herself that Toni was right. She needed to clear the air with Charles, for her own peace of mind. Still, that would have to wait. She reached for the blue plastic folder.

That afternoon Agatha drove out of Mircester along the road toward Carsely. The sun shone bright and clear in the pale-blue spring sky and newborn lambs tussled shakily with each other in the fields. The hedgerows were sprouting green, and here and there wild flowers decorated the roadside — a blush of red clover, dainty white primroses and glimpses beyond the hedges of bluebells beginning to carpet the woodland. She turned down a narrow, winding side road that led to the gates of Barfield House. The ornamental wrought-iron gates stood open, as ever, leaning drunkenly away from their hinges on the tall stone gateposts, the bottom edges buried in tall grass.

The trees that lined the long driveway eventually opened onto the landscaped lawns surrounding the house, allowing the building space to breathe. On the manicured grass stood the biggest marquee that Agatha had ever seen. Tented pavilions of various shapes and sizes were not a rare sight on Barfield's grounds. The house hosted local fairs, agricultural shows and a plethora of community events. Charles had always said that while he owned the house and the estate, they really belonged to the local people. He regarded himself as something of a caretaker — an enormously privileged caretaker, Agatha mused, but a caretaker nonetheless. Marquees, therefore, regularly graced Barfield's lawns.

There was, however, a distinct lack of grace about the monstrosity that now stood there. A team of workmen hauled on ropes and hammered at wooden stakes to secure the acres of canvas. Flags, pennants and ˈunting fluttered from every upright, and

the great round roof was a hideous seg-
mented pink-and-white candy-striped eye-
sore. It looks, Agatha thought, bringing her
car to a halt in order to gawp at the thing,
just like a . . . It is! It's a circus tent! They're
holding the wedding in a big top! How appropriate — Mary has opted to turn her
charade of a wedding into a circus! Send in
the clowns!

Agatha rolled the car onwards. Even Barfield House, the huge Victorian edifice built
in what the architect must have imagined to
be a romanticised representation of a grand
medieval mansion, did not deserve to have
the garish circus tent inflicted upon it.
Charles had always agreed with her that the
house was not particularly pleasing on the
eye, despite its multitude of mullioned
windows twinkling in the sunshine, but Agatha was aghast at the bizarre tent sprawling
on the lawn below. It simply looks awful,
she thought. It's as though the old house
has hitched up her lawn to flash her knickers. It's . . . vulgar.

She parked near the stone steps leading to
the heavy black-studded oak door that was
Barfield's main entrance. Charles seldom
used this door, and had shown Agatha many
other ways into the house, but, having arrived unannounced and uninvited, she

35

decided that this was her only option. Rather than risk her pristine nail polish with the large cast-iron knocker, she pressed the electric bell push set into the door frame. Almost immediately, she heard the familiar click of Gustav's heels crossing the polished floor of the vast hall. A combination of butler, household manager and handyman, Gustav had served Charles's father and had become almost part of the fabric of the building. Agatha knew that Charles saw him as indispensable, yet she and Gustav had always been, at best, sworn adversaries.

"Oh," said Gustav, opening the door. "It's you."

"What a pleasure it is to see you again too, Gustav," Agatha smiled. "Have you missed me?"

"Sir Charles is not at home."

"Is that not at home to me, or not at home at all?"

"He is in London, staying at his club. He and some old friends are having a stag party."

"Shame," Agatha sighed. "I was hoping to have a word with him."

"I think . . ." Gustav hesitated, glancing nervously over his shoulder. "I think you had better come in. We should talk." He reached out, grabbed her by the arm and

36

yanked her inside, marching her briskly across the enormous expanse of the hall.

"Hey, what do you think you're —"

"Shh!" Gustav hissed, raising a finger to his lips. "In here, quickly."

He opened a door near the back of the hall, close to where Agatha recalled a large, bright, modern kitchen. The door led into a long, narrow room that was little more than a corridor. Wooden panelling, cupboards and worktops flanked a central gangway that opened out to a wider room where two Belfast sinks, with tall brass taps, stood below a frosted-glass window. There was a small kitchen table and two chairs. Gustav thrust her towards one.

"What the hell are you playing at?" Agatha demanded. "You can't just drag me in here and —"

"Keep your voice down!" Gustav breathed. "The walls have ears in this house nowadays. This is the only place where it is even remotely safe for us to talk. If they knew you were here, the buggers would boot me out without a second thought."

"What *is* this place?" Agatha asked, looking around her. "And who would boot you out? The Brown-Fields?"

"It's the old butler's pantry," Gustav explained, lowering himself into the wooden chair opposite Agatha. She watched him settle and cross his legs. He moved, as he always had done, with the elegance of a dancer. He had the strength of an athlete, too. Agatha massaged the top of her arm where he had held her in a vice-like grip.

"Yes," he said grimly, "the Brown-Fields would love to have an excuse to send me packing, so we must keep this brief. I will not offer you tea."

"Gustav, what's going on?" Agatha asked. "We have never exactly been the best of friends, but I don't like to see you behaving like this. You're not acting normal."

"There is nothing normal about what's going on in this house! We may never have been friends. We may never be friends, but I know there is one thing we both genuinely care about."

"Charles."

"*Sir* Charles. He is in London, as I said. So is that obnoxious little cow he is about to marry. She is partying with her friends and having a final dress fitting. 'Miss Mary' is what she has decreed I should call her. After the wedding, it is to be 'Your Ladyship.' Can you imagine? Who does the little bitch think she is?"

"I take it her parents are here? I know ey've moved in."

"They are using a suite of rooms in the east wing as their apartment. I have been instructed to refer to them as Mr. Darell and Mz Linda. Mz? I mean, what sort of a bloody title is that? Sounds like a bee farting. These people are scum — mongrels — no breeding whatsoever."

"That's rich coming from a humble servant with a Hungarian father and an English mother," Agatha scoffed.

"You mean me?" Gustav frowned. He was notoriously secretive about his past. "Who told you my father was Hungarian?"

"Bill Wong."

"The policeman? Well, he doesn't know everything, does he? Anyway, this isn't about me. This is about Sir Charles."

"Oh bollocks!" Agatha groaned, then caught Gustav's furious look. "Not you, Gustav — them. Darell and Linda. It's Mary's middle name, isn't it? Half her father's and half her mother's — Darlinda."

"Have you only just realised? Not much of a detective really, are you?" Gustav frowned, then returned swiftly to his subject. "They are destroying Sir Charles, Mrs. Raisin. That little bitch is constantly on his back. If she's not nagging him about this outrageous wedding, she's telling him how he should run the estate — and her father

39

is always on hand to back her up. They never give him a moment's peace. I don't believe Sir Charles is actually in London celebrating his forthcoming marriage. I think he has gone there simply to get away from these dreadful people."

"Maybe he won't come back."

"He will be back. He dare not do anything to jeopardise this farce of a wedding. They have a terrible hold over him."

"So I believe," Agatha agreed, "but he wouldn't discuss it with me."

"Nor me," Gustav admitted, "and I pride myself on always having been his closest confidant."

"Your advice hasn't always been entirely welcome. You tried to poison my relationship with Charles more than once because you didn't see me as a suitable lady of the manor. I hated you for that."

"I neither expected nor required you ever to like me, Mrs. Raisin. My duty is to protect the best interests of Sir Charles Fraith."

"Well that's not been going too well over the past few months, has it? You've let the Brown-Fields start to rule the roost here at Barfield. How is his aunt taking it all?"

"Mrs. Tassy scarcely appears downstairs ˅wadays. She even takes her meals in her room. I fear this may be the end of her."

Agatha was shocked. Charles's aunt was a tall, willowy woman whose pale face and silver hair gave her the look of someone who had never been anything less than what was referred to in polite society as "a certain age." Yet Agatha knew the old lady was as strong as a horse. She hated to think of the Brown-Fields clipping her wings when she was as much a part of Barfield House as the grand staircase or the portraits in the library.

"We have to stop these devils, Mrs. Raisin!" Gustav's hands clenched into fists. "When I think of that hideous creature Sir Charles is about to marry, it makes me so angry. She struts around the house making notes about changes she will make. Oak panels to be ripped out. Furniture and rugs to be discarded. I could slap her stupid face!"

"There's a lot to slap."

"Without doubt. A chin like a sideboard."

"With the bottom drawer open."

"Honestly, I wake at night having dreamt about wringing her neck." He made a strangling motion with his hands. "We must rid Sir Charles of these utter scumbags, but I am at a loss to know how."

"Well, I doubt we can stop the wedding at this stage," said Agatha, "but marriages

41

don't last forever." She handed Gustav her business card. "Here's my number. Keep in touch. Don't do anything silly and go riding off on that motorbike of yours."

"I won't," said Gustav, calming himself. His prized Harley-Davidson had been a gift from Charles. Agatha wanted to remind him that his years of devotion to the Fraith family were appreciated and had been rewarded. She needed to use that loyalty to stop him from doing anything rash. He had once run off to work briefly in Switzerland when Charles had become engaged to some poor girl of whom he did not approve. How he had managed to keep himself under control this time was a miracle.

"I need you here," said Agatha, rising to leave. "I need you as my eyes and ears in this house. If we work together, maybe we can find a way to drag Charles out of this mess."

"Very well." Gustav directed her to a small door that led to a courtyard at the side of the house. "You had best leave this way. Less chance of you being spotted."

Once back in her car, Agatha drove past the big top and on down the avenue of trees, slowing to a halt by the main gates. She scrabbled in her bag for her mobile phone.

■ ■ ■ ■

Roy Silver was sitting in his office at Pedman PR, idly gazing out of the window at the London traffic grumbling in gridlocked paralysis three storeys below. He sipped lapsang souchong from a china cup, enjoying the smoky pine flavour of the tea and contemplating the misery of joining the turmoil of commuters to make his way home. The warm spring weather was overheating the city, and if it continued, as it was forecast to do, the fumes and dust in the streets would become unbearable.

His phone rang and he reached a languorous arm across the desk.

"Roy, it's me," came the voice of Agatha Raisin. "I need you to do something for me."

"Aggie, darling!" trilled Roy. "How lovely to hear from you. Are you enjoying the weather up there in the Cotswolds? It's becoming horribly oppressive in the city. It's playing havoc with my sinuses and it doesn't help that I am absolutely rushed off my poor little feet."

"Cut the crap, Roy. You've never done a proper day's work in your life."

"Oh, times have changed, my dear," said Roy with a forced laugh. "Since you so kindly brought me in to handle Wizz-Wazz the Donkey, I have hardly had a moment to myself."

"I doubt that very much. I know you have an entire team working on that account and that you will be raking in a fine profit from it. So you owe me, and it's payback time."

"Well, I may be able to spare a few moments. What's it all about?" Roy sighed, then suddenly perked up. "Not another juicy murder, is it?"

"No. I want you to use every London contact you have to find out what hold the Brown-Fields have over Sir Charles Fraith."

"But Aggie," complained Roy, "we've been into all of that already. The old blimps at his club and those buzzards at the banks are giving nothing away."

"Try harder, Roy. There is a contract of some sort. Tempt some young lawyer out for a drink and ply him with tequila. Tell people that you're looking to instruct new lawyers or accountants for your business and pump them for information. Twist a few arms. Cheat. Lie. Blackmail. The gloves are off. We have to know."

"That all sounds terribly serious," Roy said, his voice laced with delight at the thought of the intrigue. "I'll get on to it straight away."

44

Agatha eased her car out onto the road and set off for her cottage in Carsely. She had promised herself time and time again that she would not involve herself in Charles's affairs. He had let her down so badly. He hadn't even told her about getting engaged. How could he have treated her like that? And Gustav and Charles's aunt have snubbed me so many times, she told herself, that I really shouldn't care about them either. Yet none of them deserves Darell and Linda Brown-Field, or Mary Darlinda. I mean — Darlinda! Really? I simply can't abandon Charles, no matter what sort of trouble he's in. I have to do something!

Agatha smiled as she felt a warm glow in her chest. Now that she had committed herself, now that she was about to do battle, she felt more alive than she had done for months.

"I got us some sandwiches," said Toni, offering Agatha a choice of two paper-wrapped parcels. "Coronation chicken or ham salad?"

Agatha chose the ham salad with a nod of thanks. Bearing in mind their exchange earlier that day, she had been treading lightly ever since Toni had arrived to pick

45

her up. She had kept the tone of her voice soft and tried to maintain a calm atmosphere in the car. They were parked on a tree-lined street, which, judging by the size of the houses and the expensive cars parked in their driveways, was in a solidly affluent area of Oxford. The building opposite which Toni had parked was newer than the larger, mainly Victorian homes farther down the street, part of a terrace of four recently built compact town houses on a spacious corner plot that must at one time, Agatha surmised, have been occupied by a single mansion house. Each was three storeys, with a wooden front door standing alongside a wide garage door.

"It's the one at the end," said Toni, unwrapping her sandwich. She placed the digital camera with its long lens on the dashboard behind the steering wheel. "Patrick says the car that dropped the male visitor belongs to a local cab company. They pick up a Mr. Smith from the station, deliver him to this address and collect him later. He pays cash. I guess Smith is probably not his real name."

She tucked into her sandwich. Outside it was growing dark, and the harsh light from the street lamps was tempered only slightly by the tinted glass of the car windows. It

46

was not a flattering light, Agatha decided, yet her young companion still managed to look amazing. How could anyone look that good in this light? How could anyone look that good while she was eating a coronation chicken sandwich? Not for the first time, Agatha felt a pang of jealousy. A couple of years ago, they could have walked into a room together and she knew she would easily have stolen Toni's thunder. Now, she thought, I could diet for a week, have my hair and make-up done perfectly, wear killer heels, knockout diamonds and that sheer silk dress with the plunging neckline, and I would still be invisible next to Toni.

Toni was wearing a simple black sweater and black jeans — practical attire for this sort of work. Agatha had intended to wear a pair of black cotton trousers, but over the past few weeks a series of microwaved lasagnas, more often than not with chips and half a bottle of Merlot, meant that no matter how hard she clenched her own teeth, the teeth of her trouser zip refused to come together. The black skirt she had chosen instead was only marginally less troublesome to fasten. She nibbled at the corner of her sandwich, feeling her waistband tighten with every swallow.

"Toni," she said softly, "about earlier

today. I —"

"Don't," Toni interrupted, turning to face her. "Your apologies always sound insincere."

"What do you mean, insincere?" Agatha bristled. "My apologies are never insincere! My apologies are amongst the best in the business!"

"That's much better." Toni giggled. "That sounds more like the Agatha I know. I don't want to work for a meek and mild Agatha Raisin. That would just be too boring."

"Well." Agatha relaxed and smiled. "Let's just say we both said some things and leave it at that. Friends?"

"Friends," said Toni. "Wait — look there! That's the car!"

She grabbed the camera as a blue saloon car drew up and disgorged a single passenger, clearly male, of average height and wearing a coat with a high collar turned up. He hurried up the three steps to the front door, which was opened to allow him entry without him even breaking stride.

"That was smooth," said Toni. "I'm not surprised Simon couldn't get a photo. I've got nothing either."

"We can wait for him to come out," said Agatha, "or we can try to get a look at what's going on inside."

48

"What do you suggest?"

"We could knock on the front door posing as market researchers," Agatha said, producing an official-looking clipboard from the footwell, "though I doubt our man is going to come to the door."

"Mrs. Chadwick might," said Toni, "but it's not her we need to photograph."

"I've seen houses like these before," Agatha reasoned, "and I know the layout. Ground floor is the garage, with a kitchen/diner and living room at the back opening onto a garden area. First floor has a small bedroom at the front, a couple of bathrooms, and master bedroom at the rear. Top floor has a couple of attic bedrooms and another bathroom."

"We can assume, then, that they'll head for the master bedroom at the back."

"Let's go take a look!"

They walked up a service access path at the side of the building, picking their way through a scattering of builders' rubble and broken, discarded tools, evidence of the houses' recent completion. Toni led the way, using a carefully shielded torch to light the clutter at their feet. A high fence ran back from the rear of the building, and looking up, they could see that the only light at the back of the house was in the window of the master bedroom.

"We can't see a thing through that window from this angle," whispered Toni.

"No," Agatha agreed, "but we could use that." She pointed to a rickety ladder lying amid the builders' rubbish. Making as little noise as possible, they dragged it to the side of the building and leaned it gently against the wall.

"I'm going up," said Agatha, slinging the camera strap over her shoulder. "If I can squint round the corner, I should be able to see something and get a shot."

"Be careful, Agatha. It doesn't look very sturdy."

"It'll be fine as long as you hold on to it and check where I'm putting my feet."

Agatha made her way steadily up the ladder, thankful that she had worn shoes with sensible, although not entirely flat, heels. Halfway up, with her feet higher than her head would normally be, she began feeling nervous and looked down. Toni was gazing out into the street.

"Toni!" she hissed. "You're supposed to be watching where I put my feet!"

"But if I look up, I can see right up your skirt . . ."

"You won't see anything up there that you can't see on a rack in Marks and Spencer!"

"Yes, but on the rack it's not quite so . . . animated!"

Agatha tutted and climbed higher. Once she was level with the window, she gingerly poked her head round the corner. She had only a partial view of the room through the window, and through an open fanlight she could hear music playing — a country rock riff — and a plaintive voice singing "Saddle Up the Palomino." Then Mrs. Sheraton Chadwick strode into view. She looked to be in her early thirties and was wearing a black velvet riding helmet, black jacket with a jewelled horse brooch, white jodhpurs and gleaming black leather riding boots. She was tapping a riding crop against her thigh, a thin smile on her face.

Before Agatha lost sight of her, she distinctly heard the words, "Who's been a naughty little pony then?" And the response: "Bring it on, baby — I'm hot to trot!"

As she leaned farther over to try to see more, the ladder creaked and wobbled, and she felt the urgent need to have her feet firmly on solid ground. She made her way quickly back down and turned to talk to Toni just as the ladder toppled over sideways, landing with a mighty crash amongst the builders' rubble.

"What was that? Who's out there?" Mrs.

Chadwick had flung open a rear window. "George — fetch the shotgun!"

"Snakes and bastards!" Agatha squeaked. "RUN!"

They bolted for the car.

CHAPTER TWO

"I'm sorry, Chris, I just don't feel like going out to dinner tonight. I don't think I would be very good with lots of people around . . . I know that, but you'll have your friends there, and you'll be back before you know it. We can do something then, I promise . . . Yes, lunch would be great. You can tell me all about it then. Have a good trip. Bye." Agatha replaced the telephone handset in its cradle and slumped onto the sofa. Her two cats, Hodge and Boswell, leapt up beside her and launched into a purring contest, competing for her attention. She gently stroked both of them and they curled up on either side of her.

Chris Firkin was a very nice, kind, gentle man — and very good-looking. She was rather fond of him, and he was very keen on her. I may never find another one like him, she thought. What am I doing? He wanted to cheer me up, but I don't really want cheering up. He wanted to talk to me, but I don't really want to talk. He wanted to . . . well, one of his marathon stints in the bedroom was definitely out of the question. Gaspingly good under the right circumstances, but tonight was not the night. It was a shame that he was about to jet off on business, but Agatha simply couldn't face the impromptu get-together with friends that night.

She sat alone. It was early evening and growing dark, but her cosy cottage living room was lit by just one barely adequate table lamp. The gloom suited her mood. She was wearing a shocking-pink fluffy onesie. The one-piece pyjama garment had been bought in a post-lunch gin-fuelled shopping frenzy. Most of what she had bought, Agatha knew, would go to a charity shop after a single wearing, perhaps even box-fresh. The retail therapy had not helped to lift her spirits but the onesie was soft and comforting. She plucked at the cotton fabric of one sleeve and promised herself that she would bin it tomorrow.

The doorbell rang. She decided to ignore it. Then came a tap at the front window and the handsome face of James Lacey, her next-door neighbour and ex-husband, peered in.

"Come on, Aggie," he called. "I know

you're in there. Thought you might like a bit of company."

He held up a bottle of Sancerre and two glasses.

"I'll be right there, James!" Agatha hopped off the sofa and the cats dashed out of the room towards the kitchen. She checked her make-up in the mirror above the mantelpiece and reapplied her lipstick. She might have been wearing a garment that she wouldn't normally be seen dead in, but Agatha Raisin would never be seen — not even dead — without make-up. She crossed the cramped hallway and flung open the front door.

"Wasn't sure if I should use my key and . . . Good grief!" said James. "What on earth are you wearing?"

"I know, I know," said Agatha, walking back into the living room. "It's not really me, but I haven't been feeling much like me today."

They sat together on the sofa and James poured the wine.

"Thought you might be feeling a bit down in the dumps this evening," he said. "Can't have that, can we?"

They clinked glasses and Agatha snuggled into James. He was not, she well knew, the most affectionate or demonstrative of men, but he had a good heart.

"Want to talk about it?" he asked.

"Not especially."

So they sat in comfortable silence, sipping their wine, Agatha with her head on his chest, listening to the beating of his good heart.

"You know," she said after a while, "I sometimes think the biggest mistake we made as a couple was getting divorced."

"You may well be right," he agreed, "but it's clearly tomorrow's wedding that's making you think about it."

"I guess so," she said. "I seem to have been thinking of little else lately."

"Then we need to think of a way to get it out of your system."

"Why do you always do that?"

"Do what?"

"That typical man thing — trying to find a solution to the problem. Sometimes there isn't a practical answer. Some problems just don't have solutions."

"Well, I don't think that should stop us from trying to find them. Even if we never get to a solution, we will surely learn more about the problem."

"You sound like you're delivering one of your lectures about your travel or military history books." Agatha sat up and smiled, holding out her glass for a refill. "But thank you for trying."

"Do you still love him?"

"Charles? No, that ship sailed a long time ago. It's the whole wedding charade that I can't get out of my head. I still care about what happens to him."

"Of course you do. So why don't you go to the wedding? I shall come with you as your partner."

"Don't be silly. We haven't been invited."

"Now who's being silly?" James laughed. "When did a little thing like the lack of an invitation ever stop Agatha Raisin from doing what she wanted?"

Agatha sat up straight, her dark eyes glinting in the soft light. The Raisin brain, James realised, was ticking over.

"You need to go home," she said, trotting towards the stairs. "We don't have much time. I need to make plans. I need to think about what I'm going to wear — we're going to a wedding tomorrow!"

The path through the woods was soft underfoot, vindicating Agatha's decision to wear the green Wellington boots that were normally kept by her back door, used only for an occasional potter around the garden. They looked utterly ridiculous with her dress, but that couldn't be helped, and in any case she and James were highly unlikely to come across anyone on this woodland trail. Agatha carried shoes to change into. James was a couple of paces behind, following her through the dappled shade.

They had parked at the Huntsman, a wayside inn on the edge of the Barfield estate, where Agatha and Charles had stopped for a drink once or twice. Agatha had suggested a swift intake of Dutch courage before gatecrashing the wedding, and James had proceeded to explain that the term had originated in the seventeenth century, when soldiers drank Dutch gin to calm their fears and rouse their fighting spirit before battle. With nothing better to do just then, Agatha had listened politely while sipping her gin and tonic in the pub garden. The back of the garden led into the woods, where the path they were walking had been easy to find.

With Gustav having supplied a detailed itinerary of the day, Agatha had decided that the best time to take a look at the proceedings was late afternoon, by which time the day guests would have eaten but the evening guests would not yet have arrived. She and James were aiming to make it in time for the speeches, giving them a good opportunity to study the other guests while the attention of those in the bridal party was distracted.

Long before they reached the end of the path, they could clearly see the wedding big top overwhelming the lawn in front of Barfield House. Agatha had chosen this route in order to get close to the tent without being seen, but they still had a short stretch of grass to negotiate once they broke cover. They surveyed the scene, peering out from behind an ancient oak.

"Some of the side panels are open," James pointed out. "Must be for ventilation, but it means we might be seen."

"Maybe," said Agatha, "but look at the way they're seated." She unfolded a piece of paper from her handbag. "Gustav sent me this seating plan. The guests will be facing away from us, looking towards the top table as the speeches are delivered. They're not likely to notice us, and we won't be seen from the top table either if we approach the tent from this direction. Our only problem will be getting past him." She gestured towards a man standing near one of the open side panels, wearing a black suit and bow tie.

"Black tie?" James frowned. "Evening wear is hardly the right thing for —"

"He's not a guest, James," Agatha tutted. "Look at the way his biceps fill his sleeves. He's security."

"Security guards at a wedding?" said James. "Who are these people — the Mafia?"

"They're not well liked, that's for sure," said Agatha, "but there's no need for guards here. It's just another way for the Brown-Fields to show off, I suppose. I can deal with him. Follow my lead."

Agatha marched out onto the lawn. The bright afternoon sunshine immediately illuminated the pale blue of her dress, highlighted with an elegantly slim black trim at the round neckline and the ends of the short sleeves. She marched straight towards the tent with James in close support. At the edge of the open side flap, she paused and began hauling one foot out of its Wellie. The guard spoke firmly yet quietly, clearly briefed for today's event to use his discretion rather than his muscles.

"Excuse me, madam. Are you official wedding guests?"

"Of course we are, young man!" Agatha laughed in a shrill upper-crust accent. "We are old friends of Sir Charles."

James gave Agatha's performance an almost imperceptible nod of approval. She smiled as she cocked a leg to slip on a shiny black stiletto, and nodded back. It was his turn.

"Yes, old friends," said James. He didn't have to try quite so hard with the accent. "I was his history tutor at Cambridge, you know."

"But you look like you came from the direction of the woods," said the guard.

"Oh, it's terribly discreet in those woods," said Agatha in a hushed voice. "Perfect for a bit of . . . you know . . . outdoors rumpy-pumpy!"

The guard's eyebrows shot up. He pointed to her boots. "But you have Wellies with you . . ."

"It's a bit muddy in there, so we came prepared," Agatha explained, smoothing her hair.

"Premeditated rumpy," said James, giving the guard a wink as they breezed past into the tent.

Agatha and James accepted glasses of champagne from a tray offered to them by a waiter and picked a spot not too far from the open tent flap from where they could survey the whole of the big top. Some of the guests were, like them, standing with glasses in hand, having left their tables to chat with friends. The majority sat at round tables, each laid for eight guests, the white table-cloths crowded with wine bottles and glasses. The tables were arranged on a taut carpet of canvas ground sheets around a huge area of wood-laid dance floor. The bridal party sat, as Agatha had expected, on a slightly raised podium. An army of catering staff marching out of the tent laden with crockery and cutlery indicated that the meal was over. Agatha was not surprised that the event was running precisely to schedule. Normal weddings seldom did, but this was not a normal wedding. This was Mary Darlinda Brown-Field's wedding.

The room fell silent as a liveried master of ceremonies announced the father of the bride and Darell Brown-Field rose to speak.

"I would like to begin," he said, "by saying how proud I am of my beautiful daughter . . ."

"Which daughter's that?" whispered a woman to Agatha's left, giggling with a friend. "And why's she not here?"

Agatha turned her attention to the bride. Mary was wearing her dark hair up, with a cascade of ringlets falling to the nape of her neck. Diamond earrings dazzled above an equally impressive diamond necklace, their combined sparkle far outshining the gaudy chandeliers that hung from the ceiling of the big top. Her dress, what Agatha could see of it, was white silk, with a plunging neckline that left her arms and most of her shoulders bare. Agatha had always conceded that Mary had a good figure and wore clothes with a certain style, and her bridal outfit appeared to be no exception.

Charles was seated next to his bride. He was immaculately dressed in a crisp black morning suit, gold waistcoat and blue tie, matching the outfit worn by his father-in-law. As if he knew he was being watched, he turned his head and spotted Agatha. He forced a smile and raised his glass. The movement caught the attention of Mary, who followed his gaze and stared with disbelief. She shot a look of sheer malice across the room. Agatha calmly responded by slowly tilting her champagne glass, pouring the contents onto the canvas floor. With her father droning on, oblivious to all but the sound of his own voice, Mary gesticulated to the master of ceremonies and nodded in Agatha's direction.

"The game's up, James," said Agatha. "Time to go."

She stopped outside the tent to remove her shoes. The security guard grinned, started to say something and then froze under Agatha's thunderous glare. She hurried off towards the woods. James scooped up her Wellies, shrugged at the guard and strode after her.

That evening Agatha fed Boswell and Hodge, slipped into a light jacket and sauntered down her garden path into Lilac Lane. The lilacs after which the street was named, and which dominated most of the front gardens of her neighbours' cottages, were not quite in flower yet, but yellow daffodils bobbed their heads in the gentle breeze, complementing the golden forsythia flowers and brightening the gathering dusk. She had declined James's offer of dinner and he had retreated to his own cottage, years of experience with the notorious Raisin mood swings warning him that his company was not required.

Agatha strolled out into Carsely High Street and headed up the hill, admiring the straggle of terraced cottages, some under thatch and some with slate roofs, all with walls of yellow Cotswold stone glowing in the twilight. She passed the butcher's, the post office and the general store and carried on, pausing only when she came to the low wall surrounding the vicarage garden. As she looked up at the church steeple, towering protectively over the village, she heard her name being called.

"Agatha! Hello, my dear. How are you?"

Margaret Bloxby, the vicar's wife, was walking up the garden towards her, holding a handful of freshly cut daffodils.

"Contemplating a religious experience?" she asked, looking up towards the steeple. "It never fails to impress, I find. At any time of day, in any light, there's something warm and solid and comforting about it."

"I agree," said Agatha. "About the church steeple, I mean, not the religious experience." Then she realised she was talking to a vicar's wife. "I'm sorry . . . I don't mean that . . . Well, you know me . . ."

"Yes, I do." Mrs. Bloxby smiled, dismissing Agatha's apology with a wave of her free hand. "Why don't you come in? We can have a glass of sherry."

"Thanks," said Agatha. "I'd like that."

Mrs. Bloxby led the way into the vicarage and pointed towards the drawing room. "You know where the bottle and the glasses are kept," she said. "You pour while I pop these in a vase to cheer up Alf's study. He's at a function at his other church tonight. I managed to duck out of it."

Agatha poured their drinks and settled into an armchair beside the window. Mrs. Bloxby bustled back into the room and settled herself in a matching chair. She picked up her sherry and they clinked glasses then took a sip. Agatha looked across at a large table that was groaning under the weight of dozens of elaborately iced cakes.

"The Carsely Ladies' Society Bake Off," Mrs. Bloxby explained. "We'll be judging them after church tomorrow. There's still time to enter, if you like."

"Probably best not," said Agatha. "Who could forget the quiche incident?"

"Indeed," Mrs. Bloxby said. "Murder and mayhem. You have certainly spiced up our lives since arriving in Carsely, Agatha. I was thinking of you today. The wedding, of course. Wondering how you were coping with it all. Sounds like it was a sumptuous affair."

"It was. I was there."

"Really? I shouldn't have thought Sir Charles's bride would have agreed to you being invited."

"She didn't. I wasn't exactly invited. I just felt I had to see it for myself."

"You gatecrashed the wedding of the year!" Mrs. Bloxby laughed. "That's wonderful! I shall look out for you in the background when the photos appear in those society magazines. What is it the youngsters call it nowadays — 'photo bombing'?"

"I doubt I'll be in any photos." Agatha smiled. "I wasn't there for very long. I wanted to see him and . . ."

"Let him know you still care?" said Mrs. Bloxby, who had had enough fireside chats with Agatha to appreciate the depth of her feelings for Sir Charles Fraith. She had had similar chats with Sir Charles. She'd got through a lot of sherry over the years.

"I do still care," said Agatha. "Not in a romantic way. Not any more. But he has been a big part of my life and I hate to see him being treated like this."

"He's still in a bad situation, then?"

"It seems worse than ever. I want to find a way to help him, but I know she'll try to stop me. I'm really not sure what I can do. Sometimes I feel totally out of my depth. Maybe I should turn my back on all of this — forget about Charles, forget about Carsely, forget it all and head back to London."

"That would be a shame, Agatha," said Mrs. Bloxby. "You would be sorely missed, and I think you know you would never forgive yourself for running away. But you don't really mean it anyway, do you? You're not a quitter."

"You're right," Agatha agreed. "There are

lots of people here I really like and just one, at the moment, that I really hate."

"Then you should concentrate on the people you like."

"I will — but first I need to deal with the one who's really pissing me off: Lady Mary Fraith."

"So the battle lines are drawn." Mrs. Bloxby sipped her sherry. "It is always very awkward trying to involve oneself in whatever goes on between a husband and wife."

"Not for a private detective," said Agatha. "It's pretty much my professional stock in trade."

"Mine too." Mrs. Bloxby smiled. "Alf writes a great sermon and is very good at organising church functions, but I do quite a bit of what you might call pastoral care."

"Does that generally involve sherry and a chat?"

"You're different," said Mrs. Bloxby, refilling their glasses. "And thank heavens for that. Sir Charles Fraith would be lost without you, and one day I'm sure he will have cause to be grateful that you were there for him — that you never gave up."

"I never will," Agatha agreed, and they clinked glasses again. "I never give up."

Had Agatha harboured any lingering doubts

about helping Charles to deal with his new wife and in-laws, they evaporated early the following afternoon. She had slept late and was showered, dressed and enjoying a cup of coffee in her kitchen, browsing the Sunday papers, when the doorbell rang. She made her way along the narrow hall to the front door, congratulating herself on having done her hair and applied make-up at leisure prior to having a visitor, whoever it might be. To her surprise, she found Mary standing on the doorstep. She was wearing a casual sweater, jeans and the kind of boots that country ladies keep for walking Labradors.

"Well, well," said Agatha, crossing her arms and leaning on the doorpost to make it clear that her visitor would not be invited inside. "The blushing bride. Shouldn't you be on honeymoon or something?"

"All in good time," Mary replied, looking up at Agatha. There was only one step up to the front door of the cottage, but Agatha was enjoying having the strategic advantage of looking down on Mary from the higher ground. "We fly out tomorrow to spend some time at our property in Spain," Mary continued, "before taking a short cruise on a rather exclusive liner. I wanted some time after the wedding to clear up a few loose ends."

"I'm not sure I like being called a loose end."

"I don't care what you like!" growled Mary. "I'm here to tell you to keep your nose out of my business. I saw you yesterday."

"I saw that you saw me yesterday."

"And the security guard told me what you were up to in the woods — with him!" Mary pointed to her right, where James was sitting on a wooden bench by his front door, enjoying the sunshine, a cup of tea and a book.

"Afternoon, James," called Agatha.

"Afternoon, Aggie."

"You really shouldn't believe everything you hear from an over-muscled cretin in an ill-fitting suit," said Agatha, "but I do hope it didn't entirely spoil your big day, Darlinda."

"It's Lady Mary to you!"

"I think not, Your Majesty. I prefer Darlinda, although it's a shame they didn't make it Lindarell, isn't? Your mother's quite pretty. With her name first, you might have inherited her looks instead of getting that," she pointed at Mary's chin, "from your old man."

70

"I don't have to take that sort of talk from you! You're not fit to scrape the shit off my shoes. I can buy and sell your sort, so tread very carefully, you old cow — and keep your fat arse off my property!"

Agatha blinked. A cold, blank look came over her face.

"Old? *Fat?*"

She shot out a hand, clutching Mary around the throat. Mary squealed and grabbed two fistfuls of Agatha's hair. In an instant, James had vaulted the low picket fence between the front gardens and prised the two women apart.

"That's enough!" he shouted. "Calm down, both of you!"

Neighbours cleaning cars in the street or tidying their flower beds craned their necks to see what was disturbing the peace on their Sunday afternoon.

"Did you see that?" Mary screeched, rubbing her throat and appealing to Agatha's neighbours. "Did you all see that? She tried to strangle me!"

"Why don't you bugger off back to Barfield House," Agatha roared, "before I finish the job?"

She stepped back into her cottage and slammed the door. Mary turned on her heel and stomped off down the garden path.

71

James let out a breath of relief and returned to his bench.

Sir Charles Fraith sat at his desk in the library of Barfield House. Of all the rooms in the house, and there were many — he had long forgotten exactly how many — this was his favourite. It was his haven, a sanctuary where he could work, think or simply sit and read. One wall of the oak-panelled room was lined with shelves of books, an ornate mahogany wheeled staircase standing ready, as it had done for over a century, to allow access to the highest levels. There were many valuable first editions among the hundreds of books, and many volumes that he treasured. He had read only a fraction of them and doubted he would manage to peruse them all during his lifetime. Some he knew well, especially those pertaining to his Cambridge history degree; others he only discovered when the mood took him to browse the collection.

Opposite the shelves were tall windows that flooded the room with light — although the shafts of direct sunlight stretched across the floor only as far as the base of the bookcases, a deliberate design to protect the spines of the volumes — and a set of French doors leading onto the terrace. In front of his desk, beyond a sofa, a pair of wing-backed chairs and a low coffee table, was a cavernous fireplace with a carved marble surround. A huge gilt-framed mirror stood proudly on the mantelpiece. Behind him the wall was dedicated to portraits of his ancestors, or at least those paintings he liked. When he had inherited the house, some had not been to his taste and were banished to rarely visited rooms or wrapped in blankets in the attic. One of those had been of Cater Thompson, a disturbing portrait that had haunted Charles's childhood. Thompson was not a direct ancestor but had owned the original Tudor house that had once stood where Barfield now was. That house had burned down, which was hardly surprising given everything that had gone on within its walls. Thompson had been a member of a Hellfire Club and had held black mass ceremonies and ritual orgies in the house.

The portraits that remained all meant something to Charles and he knew the history and achievements of each individual. What, he wondered, shuffling invoices and payment sheets, would be counted among his achievements? Who would look at his likeness and recite his history? Would this room, this house, survive to host his portrait one day? It wasn't something to which he had ever given much consideration in the past, but now . . .

The reason for his musing made a sudden appearance, flinging open the library door.

"Have you been through those latest spreadsheets?" Mary demanded.

"I have started looking through them," Charles replied.

"They don't make very encouraging reading, do they? Take a look at the five-year projections on . . . Oh for goodness' sake! Why do you still not have a computer or even a laptop in here?"

"The computers are in the office."

"But you spend your time in here! Things are going to change in this house, Charles — get used to it."

"Things have already changed," said Charles, running his hand through his hair, "but some of the things you are proposing are entirely impractical."

"You're talking about your precious tenants again, aren't you?"

"The tenants are vital to holding the estate together, but most of the farmers and small businesses are struggling right now. They can't afford the huge rent increases you want. For some, a modest increase might be manageable, but you can't burden them with unreasonable rent hikes."

"Don't you dare tell me what I can and cannot do!" hissed Mary, stabbing a finger in Charles's direction. "Unreasonable? You haven't imposed a reasonable increase for years. If they can't pay up, they can move out!"

"Some of these people have been here for generations. I grew up with them — I won't let you kick them out. You will ruin the estate."

"Ruin the estate? I will do whatever the hell I like with the estate! Get in my way and I will ruin *you*!"

Charles watched his young wife march out of the library and slam the door behind her. He let out a low groan and sat back in his chair. She was passionate about making money. She was passionate about show-jumping with her bloody horses. If only she had brought some of that passion into the bedroom. Their wedding night had not been what one would call an unqualified success. He had hoped that sleeping together would mellow her aggressive nature, but all she had done was complain that he was hurting her. That was particularly upsetting as Charles had always prided himself on being a gentle and sensitive lover. Perhaps things would change when they were on honeymoon.

His thoughts were interrupted by a knock at the door, and Gustav entered.

"Bags are packed for your package holiday to the Brown-Field bungalow," he announced.

"It's not a package holiday, Gustav," said Charles, "it's our honeymoon. And it's a villa near Marbella, not a bungalow."

"Does it have an upstairs?"

"No."

"Then it's a bungalow."

"I wish you would try to be a bit more accommodating towards these people, Gustav. They are going to be a permanent feature around here, not just weekend guests."

"You need to see this." Gustav spoke quietly as he approached the desk. He reached furtively into an inside jacket pocket and handed Charles a folded sheet of paper. Charles's eyes widened as he scanned the document.

"Where did you get this?" he gasped.

"Where'd you think? Off her desk."

"The bitch! I'll kill her! I swear it — I'll kill her!"

CHAPTER THREE

"He had calmed down a bit by the time I took them to the airport this morning, but it doesn't bode well for a successful honeymoon, does it?"

"Your timing was pretty poor, Gustav," said Agatha, holding her phone in one hand while stroking Hodge with the other. She was sitting in the sunshine in her back garden, the cat curled up in her lap. Boswell was crouched on the grass staring intently at nothing at all in the shadows beneath a hydrangea. "Charles has been so stressed that it might have been kinder at least to give him a chance to relax while he's away. You could have waited."

"Would you have waited?"

"I might have," Agatha lied.

"Bullshit," Gustav cursed. "Whose side are you on? This is a dirty war and we have to fight dirty."

"All right," said Agatha. "I need to see

this document. Can you photograph it with your phone and send it to me?"

"Already done," said Gustav and hung up.

Agatha lifted Hodge off her lap and set him down on the grass beside Boswell. He joined in the staring for a moment, then swiped the other cat on the head with a paw before scampering off with Boswell hot on his heels. Agatha stared at her phone. Gadgets and electronic gizmos were not her strong suit, but she was sure she could retrieve Gustav's photo if she just thought about it for a second or two.

"Not working today?" James's head appeared above the hedge between the gardens.

"Late start," Agatha explained. "Toni's coming to pick me up and we're going to talk to a woman who thinks she has a poltergeist."

"Spooky." James smiled. "But you have to take these things seriously around here. There are plenty of locals who still believe in witches, fairies and ghosts."

"I know," Agatha agreed. "I've come across quite a few of them. James, would you be a sweetheart and help me with this wretched phone?"

"Of course. Why don't you come round? I've just made a fresh pot of coffee."

They sat together drinking coffee at a small table in James's neat garden. James tapped and swiped at Agatha's phone and then handed it back to her.

"The document is there on your screen. Just tap to open it," he said. "The text will be quite small but you should be able to read it."

"Thank you, James," said Agatha. "You know, I've been thinking about what we were saying the other night. About us being too hasty about the divorce."

"I have, too," James admitted, "and I came to the conclusion that when we got married I was an old bachelor, set in my ways, maybe not prepared for the changes that marriage would bring. In your own way, perhaps you were too."

"I think you're right," said Agatha, "apart from the 'old' bit. So that's something else we agree on — something else we have in common."

She looked at her phone and tapped the icon on the screen. The document that opened was headed "Barfield House Luxury Hotel and Spa." She stared at it, her mouth set in a grimace.

"Are you all right, Aggie?" asked James. "Bad news?"

A car horn sounded in the street.

"That must be Toni," said Agatha, getting to her feet. "I have to go."

"Well don't let the ghosties scare you too much," he joked, and stooped to give her a peck on the cheek. They embraced, holding each other in a hug for a heartbeat or two, then Agatha backed away and smiled.

"Let's talk more later," she said.

"Yes," said James. "Let's do that."

Toni was sitting waiting behind the wheel of her little car when Agatha jumped into the passenger seat. The windows were open and Toni was wearing a flower-patterned summer dress and sunglasses. Her arms were bare.

Agatha smoothed the skirt of her own forest-green suit, settling the hem just above her knee. She had always had good legs and knew how best to show them off with skirts and heels that worked together to flatter their shape. Her concession to the warm spell of weather had been to abandon tights, shave her legs with particular care and apply a light touch of fake tan — not enough to imply a leisurely fortnight spent lazing in the Mediterranean sun, but just sufficient to banish the pallid winter hue. Toni clearly knew nothing about preparing for the seasons. She had jumped into that dress as soon as the sun came out, but because she was naturally slim and pretty, anything she wore looked great. Agatha pursed her lips and gave her a sideways look.

"That outfit's a bit summery, isn't it?" she said.

"Do you think so?" said Toni. "It's just that the weather has been so warm. I can dash home for something else if you like, but I felt like I wanted something different. I needed a change."

"A change . . ." Agatha mused. "Yes, of course you did. We all need a change now and again, don't we? You don't need to dash home, Toni, you look fabulous."

"And you look very elegant, as always," said Toni. "You look like the boss, like you're in control."

"That's just as it should be," said Agatha as they set off. She closed the car window, despite the heat of the sun scorching through the windscreen. Toni gave her a quizzical look and Agatha made a wind-rush gesture against the window.

"Ruins the hair," she said, "and gives you the complexion of a round-the-world sailor."

Pulling out onto the A44, they joined light traffic heading north-west towards Moreton-in-Marsh. Prior to snapping up her cottage in Carsely, Agatha had considered moving to Moreton. It was an ancient market town, a settlement having existed on the site for more than two thousand years, yet it seemed somehow more modern than Carsely. The scattering of thatched roofs that graced a few of the buildings in the centre of Carsely were nowhere to be seen in Moreton. The buildings there were of the same mellow Cotswold stone but the roofs were all either stone tiles or slate. Moreton was also bigger than Carsely, yet it still retained the undeniable charm that had lured Agatha away from the glitz and clamour of London life.

As they passed the inevitable clusters of galleries and antique shops, the impressive flank of the Redesdale Market Hall loomed in front of them. Agatha checked her watch against the nineteenth-century black-and-white clock face on the tower that crowned the hall and decided that one of them was not quite right. She cast an eye at the black-and-gold face of the even older clock on the Curfew Tower to their right. That was also slightly different. She opted to back her battery power against the ancient clocks. The differences, after all, were minimal.

Turning right, they headed up the high street past the Black Bear Inn. To the left of the wide thoroughfare was the market area, giving way to an avenue of trees and the imposing presence of the Old Police Station, which the police had long since surrendered to private residences. The high street was very straight, as was the road they turned onto, heading towards Batsford.

"This is all very pretty," said Toni, admiring the trees that were now almost in full leaf at either side of the road, and the public park rolling into fields that looked lush and green in the spring sunshine. "It's an incredibly straight road."

"An old Roman road," said Agatha. "They knew the quickest route was the straightest route, so they didn't bother much with curves and corners. I think we turn off to the left here."

They pulled off the main road onto a farm track that led to a stone-built farmhouse with a tiled gabled roof, dormer windows nestling just below the ridge line. The car tyres crunched on the stone-chip driveway and Toni parked by a bed of roses that decorated the front of the house. Agatha stepped gingerly out of the car. She hated stone chips. They destroyed delicate high heels. Toni strode forward and rang the doorbell.

"Mrs. Jessop?" said Agatha to the woman

who opened the door. "I'm Agatha Raisin, and this is my associate Toni Gilmour."

"Oh, I *am* pleased to see you." Mrs. Jessop gave them a welcoming smile and shook their hands. "Please, do come in." She led them along the hallway towards the back of the house.

She looks, thought Agatha, in good shape. Probably mid to late sixties, slim build, about the same height as myself, well dressed in a neat cardigan and tweed skirt, carefully coiffured hair and modest make-up. This is not the shambling old wreck I expected. She seems quite robust — not the sort to go to pieces over hearing a few bumps in the night.

"Come into the kitchen," said Mrs. Jessop. "This is where I've been having the problem. Would you like some tea?"

"That would be lovely," said Agatha.

The kitchen was clearly newly fitted, with plenty of wall and base unit cupboards and marble work surfaces arranged around a large wooden kitchen table with six high-backed wooden chairs. Agatha and Toni sat at the table while Mrs. Jessop reached up to open a cupboard door. She hesitated.

"There, you see?" she said. "This is what I'm talking about. This is where I keep the tea caddy and cups, and now they've gone."

84

She opened and closed a few more doors, then crossed to the other side of the kitchen and did the same until she finally found the tea.

"I know it seems silly," she said, busying herself with a kettle and teapot, "but things in these cupboards are being moved about. I sort it all out just the way I like it, and when I next open a cupboard, it has all changed!"

"How annoying," said Agatha. "That would drive me crazy."

"Oh, I'm not crazy, Mrs. Raisin," Mrs. Jessop assured her. She set a china teapot on the table, along with cups, a milk jug and sugar bowl. "Something very strange is going on around here — something very sinister."

"You said when we spoke on the phone that you believed you were being visited by a poltergeist," said Toni. "Have you seen this ghost?"

"Yes, I've seen him all right," Mrs. Jessop admitted. "As plain as you can see me."

"Did you see him in the kitchen?" Agatha asked.

"No, he comes in here at night to do his mischief."

"So where have you spotted him?" asked Toni.

"Out there," said Mrs. Jessop, pointing to the large window that looked out over a stone-chip garden path, beautifully maintained flower beds bursting with spring colour and an immaculate lawn. "In the garden. That is his place, after all."

"You talk like you know who he is," said Agatha.

"Oh, I do," Mrs. Jessop replied, reaching into her cardigan pocket to produce a slightly faded, lightly creased black-and-white photograph. It showed herself as a much younger woman, standing beside a powerfully built man wearing jeans, boots and a checked shirt. He had wavy dark hair, a full beard and, even in this old photo, the most captivating eyes Agatha had ever seen. She could not imagine them to be anything other than a sharp, electric blue.

"Who is this?" Toni asked.

"You mean who *was* this," Mrs. Jessop corrected her. "That is John Cornish, my gardener. He died twenty-five years ago."

"And he's been . . . appearing in your garden?" Toni swallowed hard, staring wide-eyed at the photo. Agatha frowned at her, a clear signal to man up.

"Regular as clockwork," said Mrs. Jessop. There was the unmistakable crunch of boots on stone chips. "That," she whispered, "will be him now . . ."

The heavy tread grew louder, subduing all other sounds. The three women sat perfectly still, holding their breath, as the figure of a man drifted into view outside the window — dark wavy hair, a full beard and a checked shirt. He stopped, turning slowly towards them. Agatha felt a paralysing chill run down her spine as he fixed her with eyes of such a startling, intense blue that she could not break his gaze. An instant later, he turned away, resuming a steady pace until he was out of sight beyond the window. A blanket of silence smothered the kitchen. A tear came to Mrs. Jessop's eye and Toni was sitting bolt upright, pale and frozen to the spot.

"Snakes and bastards!" cried Agatha, jumping to her feet. "I'm not having this!" She grabbed the photograph and headed for the back door. Ignoring the stone chips scuffing the heels of her shoes, she stomped out into the garden, where she spotted the figure just a few yards ahead of her.

"Hey, you!" she called. "John Cornish! What are you doing here?"

The figure turned to face her. She avoided his eyes and stood her ground even as she felt her knees begin to fold.

"Doin' the garden, ain't I?" said Cornish.

"What's it to you?"

"I am Agatha Raisin, private investigator."

"What you got to investigate in my garden?" said Cornish, walking towards her.

"This!" said Agatha, holding up the photograph.

"Where'd you get that?" Cornish asked. "That's my old dad with Auntie Joan."

"Your father?" said Agatha, with a sigh of relief. "You're not dead, then?"

"Is that what she's been tellin' you?" Cornish laughed, stroking his beard. "Think I'd better shave this off. Beards is trendy nowadays, right? Makes me look the spitting image of my old man, though. He'd be about my age in that photo. Taught me all I know about gardens, he did."

"She really does think you are him."

"Ah." Cornish nodded. "Things ain't always what they seem, eh?"

"She thinks you're a ghost who sneaks in at night and rearranges her cupboards."

"Ah," Cornish repeated. "I should 'ave guessed. Kitchen's new. She keeps forgettin' where she put things. Auntie Joan's not been herself recently."

"She's your aunt?"

"Not really, but I grew up around this house, what with my dad workin' here. She liked me to call her auntie and always treated us like family. Uncle Tom did the same until he passed a couple of years back and left her on her own. Suppose that's when she started to lose it."

"She seems perfectly all right. She doesn't seem confused at all."

"Like I said — things ain't always what they seem. Do me a favour, would you? Keep her occupied for a little while an' I'll sneak indoors to the bathroom and get rid of this." He tugged at his beard.

Agatha headed back inside. After a few minutes spent reassuring Mrs. Jessop and Toni that there was no ghost stalking the garden, Cornish breezed into the kitchen, freshly shaved.

"Auntie Joan!" he called. "Any more tea in that pot? I'm parched."

"Of course, John!" Mrs. Jessop's face lit up at the sight of him. "You'll be wanting a biscuit or two, I should think. I've got your favourites . . . somewhere."

"Don't worry, Mrs. Raisin." Cornish winked a sparkling blue eye at Agatha. "I'm round here most days. I'll look after her."

The tale of the ghostly gardener kept everyone at Raisin Investigations amused over the following days. There was a spate of practical jokes, mostly aimed at Toni, Aga-

89

tha not being well renowned for tolerating jokes at her expense: spring-loaded spooks popping out of her desk drawers and eerie messages from the spirit world appearing on her computer screen. The pranks, Agatha knew, were perpetrated by Simon, but he appeared to have cleared up the phantom dumper case, promising to have his report ready for the next catch-up meeting, and was throwing himself into whatever other work came his way, so she allowed the fun to run its course. She had Toni find out about Mrs. Jessop's circumstances, and since she appeared to be a woman of means, she ordered a bill to be prepared for their time. "Business is business," she reminded herself, although somehow she never quite got round to sending the bill to Mrs. Jessop.

Agatha had spent the morning at home, sifting through paperwork at the kitchen table and mulling over yet another conversation she had had with James the previous evening about rekindling their relationship. She knew that she was leading him, having been the one who had first raised the matter, but he didn't seem at all reluctant to follow. But what, she thought, do I really want? Is this thing with James just a reaction to what Charles has done? What would Charles have to say about it? She could practically hear his voice.

"Hello, Aggie."

She *could* hear his voice! She looked up to see the lithe figure of Sir Charles Fraith standing in her kitchen. He was, as always, immaculately dressed. His crisp pale-yellow short-sleeved shirt showed off his sun-bronzed face and arms and his fine fair hair had taken on golden Mediterranean high-lights. At one time the sight of him looking as handsome as he did at that moment might have set Agatha's pulse racing. She was strangely disappointed that all she now felt was mild annoyance at the intrusion.

"How did you get in?" she demanded.

"Keys," he said, holding up the spare set Agatha had given him sometime in the distant past.

"Aren't you on your honeymoon?"

"Got back last night."

"What do you want?"

"Look, after all that's happened, I can understand you feeling a bit frosty towards me, sweetie —"

"Don't call me that."

"All right, all right. I just wanted to say how sorry I am for everything — and to apologise for Mary coming round here before we left. I heard about the fracas you had. I would promise that it won't happen

91

again, but I really have no control over her whatsoever. Quite frankly, she is driving me mad."

"I can imagine," said Agatha, watching him run his hand through his hair. That was a bad sign — a telltale Fraith trait that meant he was feeling particularly stressed, anxious and upset. "Sit down." She sighed. "You look like you could use a drink."

They were sitting with glasses of gin and tonic, beginning to relax into each other's company, Charles relating ever more disturbing stories of his young wife's outrageous behaviour, when the doorbell rang. Agatha opened the front door to find Chris Firkin standing on the step.

"Chris!" she said. "You're back."

"I am indeed." He grinned. "Are you ready to go?"

"Go?" Agatha asked. "Go where?"

"Lunch — I promised you lunch as soon as I got back and . . ." The smile faded from his face when he spotted Charles standing in the hallway.

"Hello, Chris." Charles nodded. Agatha sensed a distinct awkwardness between the two men. "Don't mind me, old chap. I was just leaving."

He brushed past Agatha and Chris, pausing on the garden path for a moment.

"Thank you for listening, Aggie," he said. "Let's stay in touch."

"What was all that about?" Chris asked, stepping into the hall.

"Oh, nothing," Agatha said. "He's just having a few problems with —"

"His tenants? That doesn't surprise me. I've just been hit with a massive rent increase for the workshop I rent on his estate."

"I think that's more to do with his wife than with Charles."

"Whatever. It's all part of the decision that I've made to —"

"Agatha, darling, are you there? It's about last night." James had skipped over the garden fence and appeared in the doorway. "Oh, I'm sorry. I didn't realise you had company. I'll talk to you some other time."

James made himself scarce and Agatha turned to Chris again.

"You were saying?" she asked. "What decision?"

"The decision to go," Chris explained. "This is what I've been trying to talk to you about. You know I've been doing all this work with electric cars? Well, I've been offered the chance to work with some of the best engineers in the field. It's the opportunity of a lifetime."

"That's wonderful, Chris!" Agatha congratulated him.

"It's like a dream come true for me," he said, "and I want you to be part of it. Come with me, Agatha. Come with me to California."

"California? Are you serious?"

"Never more so." He clasped Agatha's hands. "This is a chance for both of us to start a whole new life. Please say you'll think about it."

"I don't need to think about it."

"So it's a yes?" Chris's eyes were bright with jubilation.

"No, Chris," said Agatha. "It's a no. You are a lovely man and I am very fond of you, but I don't need to start a whole new life. I did that when I left London. My life is here now. I have responsibilities and —"

"James and Charles," Chris interrupted, crestfallen. "I should have known I couldn't compete with them."

"You don't need to compete with them, Chris. I'm here because I chose to be here, not because of either of them. Maybe, now and then, I still have the odd doubt about whether I belong here, and I don't know if I will ever truly fit in, but I will never give up trying. This is my home. California is not for me." She put her arms round him and held him tight, whispering, "I'm so sorry."

He looked into her eyes and smiled. "That's it then," he said, and walked off down the garden path. He did not look back, and she knew she would never see him again.

She sauntered back into the kitchen. She and Charles had not finished their drinks. She was about to pour them away when she shrugged, combined both in one glass and sat down at the table. Why, when what she so regularly longed for was a settled life with a decent man, did she now have three knocking on her door in one day? She took a swig from the glass. Men had such poor timing. Her phone rang. It was Gustav. Typical, thought Agatha — the prince of poor timing, right on cue.

"Has Sir Charles visited you today?"

"Yes, he left some time ago. Why?"

"Did he mention the party?"

"I guess he didn't get round to it. What party?"

"It's that bloody woman again. She's throwing a huge party here at the house. A masked ball, would you believe? She's celebrating her birthday with a three-day event — a restaurant binge in London, followed by a day's shooting here and then a masked ball with the theme 'Versailles.' "

"Sounds like fun."

"Fun? Are you insane? We are to be having two dozen guests for the shoot. There's nothing in season at the moment, so they'll be shooting clays, and you know what a mess that makes. They'll be staying here for two nights, with a further seventy attending the party. And she didn't say a word about it to me! A hundred guests at a damn-fool costume-and-mask fiasco!"

"Party pooper," said Agatha, taking another swig. "When's it all happening?"

"This weekend! There are decorators here now, pimping up the ballroom, and the caterers have started delivering their gear already."

"I doubt I'll get an invitation," Agatha reasoned, "but it would be a shame to miss it. Could be a good chance to check out some of her friends. Can you get me in?"

"Of course."

"Good. We'll talk later in the week."

As soon as Agatha hung up on Gustav, she poured the remains of her drink down the sink and phoned Toni at the office.

"What are you doing on Saturday? No plans? Good — keep it that way. Meet me in the King Charles opposite the office in half an hour. There's a theatrical costume hire place in Steventon. We need to pop down and have a chat with them."

On the day of the party, Toni arrived at Agatha's cottage in the late afternoon. Their visit to the costume outfitters earlier in the week had been enormously entertaining but also a valuable learning experience. They knew that they would not be able to get into their imitation seventeenth-century gowns without each other's help. Having wrestled with buttons, zips, fasteners and ties to get dressed, they retreated to separate bedrooms to work on their make-up and finishing touches.

Agatha was ready first and waited for Toni downstairs in the living room. She took a look at herself in the mirror above the fireplace. Her hair, actually a wig that fitted like a guardsman's helmet, was a cascade of brown curls sitting on top of her head and making her appear nearly a foot taller. Her face was powdered almost white, with dark liner accentuating her eyes and lipstick of a shockingly vibrant red that she would never normally dream of wearing. The pale make-up faded gently on her neck, around which she wore a triple string of fake pearls. A flourish of white lace trimmed the long sleeves and neckline of her tight royal-blue bodice, which was cut square and low, pushing her breasts into a daring display of cleavage. Below the bodice, layer upon layer of gold skirt, etched with a flower pattern, descended to trail the floor at her feet. She gave herself a nod of approval, noting with satisfaction that the wig gripped her head tightly enough not to wobble. She hitched her bosom up slightly and turned just as her assistant walked into the room.

Toni had arranged her long blonde hair in golden ringlets that swept her shoulders. She had naturally pale skin and wore little make-up save for a light-pink lipstick and a stick-on mole on her upper lip. Agatha touched a tentative finger to her own upper lip, still tender from the vicious waxing she had given it earlier in the day. At her age, she had to pay a painful price for a smooth complexion, and wondered if that was something Toni could ever understand, gifted as she was with alabaster skin and a hair-free face. Toni's gown was similar to Agatha's but in contrasting tones of pink. She looks like a true princess, thought Agatha, while I look like a pantomime dame!

"Wow! You look brilliant!" said Toni, glancing down at her chest. "I'm really not as well equipped to wear these dresses as you are . . ."

"Not at all," said Agatha, buoyed by the compliment. "You look sensational. That mole will come off again, won't it? We need to wear these as well, of course. Can't afford to be recognised." She handed Toni a sequinned eye mask. Their masks tied behind their heads with silk ribbons. Others, she knew, might have masks mounted on slim sticks that could be held in front of the face or whisked aside as the wearer chose, but the clandestine nature of their party intrusion meant that they needed permanent disguises.

As their taxi pulled up near the grand entrance to Barfield House, they could see a line of guests queuing patiently on the stone steps to be admitted. Most of the ladies were dressed in a similar fashion to Agatha and Toni. The men sported long wigs of waves and curls, and flamboyant coats that reached almost to their knees with lace cuffs that hung even lower. Knee breeches, stockings and fancy shoes were the order of the day and most wore outfits perfectly suited to the occasion. Agatha did spot a couple of Elizabethans, who were slightly out of time, and even a pirate, but all the guests could be given credit for entering into the spirit of things.

"Gustav is on the door, checking the invitations, just as he said he would be," said Toni in a hushed voice.

"You sent him our photo," said Agatha, "so he'll recognise us. Watch for his signal."

They approached the queue and could immediately hear the cause of the hold-up. A distraught young woman was searching her handbag for her invitation and pleading with Gustav to fetch Mary, who would vouch for the fact that she was a bona fide guest. Gustav was taking fiendish delight in refusing to do so and barring her entrance. He spotted Agatha and Toni about to join the end of the queue and nodded to the side. Agatha gave him a surreptitious thumbs-up.

"Let's take a walk in the grounds until all that fuss dies down," she said in a loud voice, leading Toni off towards the side of the house. "The butler's pantry," she added softly. "Gustav has left the door unlocked for us."

Having come through the butler's pantry to the rear of the hall, they entered the ballroom through the smaller side door. Mary was greeting her guests at the double doors approached from the main part of the hall. Her outfit was far grander than either Agatha's or Toni's, her hairpiece decorated with costume jewellery, her purple bodice studded with glittering fake gems and trimmed with silvery silk, the skirt a sea of rolling purple silk waves. Charles was standing close by, dressed more like a footman than the lord of the manor. Mary's father was also in attendance, his long dark wig, gold coat, gold breeches, white stockings and white shoes decorated with gold bows far outshining his son-in-law. Behind his mask, Charles looked achingly awkward. Agatha tried not to smile at his obvious discomfort and the way that Darell had positioned himself to deny him the opportunity to slope off and sulk in his beloved library. She had to try harder to spot Mary's mother, but eventually recognised her drifting elegantly among the other guests.

The ballroom had, Agatha recalled, many mirrors and a fine Venetian crystal chandelier, but it had been dressed for the evening with printed drapes hanging like tapestries. The glass doors leading to the lawn were open but manned by the same black-suited security staff who had been in attendance at the wedding circus. Up in the minstrels' gallery a small orchestra was playing, and down by the fireplace the catering staff were building a pyramid of coupe glasses for a champagne fountain beside a white-clothed table with a banner above it that read "Sun King Burger Bar." Round tables and seats surrounded the main dance floor, with more tables outside on the patio.

Agatha plucked two glasses of champagne from a tray carried by a passing flunkey and handed one to Toni.

"We are here to have a bit of fun," she said, raising her glass, "but we are also here to mix with Mary Darlinda's friends and find out whatever we can that might possibly be of use to us. So don't go dousing yourself in champagne and drawing attention to yourself."

"No, boss," said Toni, clinking Agatha's glass and saluting. "But you have to admit, this does look like fun. I've never been to a party like this before. It's incredible."

"Like I say," said Agatha. "Keep a low profile."

They mingled with other guests, exchanging pleasantries, the room slowly filling with a glittering array of fabulously dressed ladies and extravagantly attired gentlemen. Then the orchestra struck a chord and launched into a waltz. Agatha prided herself on being an excellent dancer and knew that the Strauss waltz being played by the orchestra was around a century too young for a Versailles party, although the dance itself could trace its roots back much farther. Mary and her father took to the floor, waltzing with more confidence than competence, and the other guests gradually joined in, most managing only a fair interpretation of a waltz.

Suddenly a masked young man, tall and slim, was standing in front of Agatha. He took her hand and bowed, an invitation to dance. A young man was choosing her rather than Toni! Agatha handed her champagne to her assistant, grinned, stuck out her tongue and glided off onto the dance floor.

Her partner danced reasonably well, managing to avoid tromping either on Agatha's toes or on the bottom of her dress. She found that she was leading him rather than him being in charge, but she was enjoying herself nonetheless. He was wearing rather too much of an over-perfumed aftershave, as young men tended to do. Agatha thought that it might suit her more than it did him. Then Toni spun past in the arms of a man Agatha instantly recognised — Charles! He stopped, tapped the young man on the shoulder, and they exchanged partners.

"How on earth did you two get in?" He laughed as they stepped and swirled around the crowded dance floor.

"Easy," said Agatha. "I managed to gate-crash the wedding. I certainly wasn't going to miss out on this."

"Stop!" a voice screeched. "Stop!" The music stopped. The dancers stopped. A hand clawed at Agatha's shoulder and spun her round. It was Mary.

"It's you!" she howled, reaching out and ripping off Agatha's mask. "I knew it! I warned you to stay away!"

"I invited her!" Charles lied.

"Well I'm UN-inviting her!" Mary growled, stepping quickly forward and planting the heels of her hands in Agatha's chest with a mighty thump. The shove sent Agatha stumbling backwards. She crashed into the champagne fountain just as the catering manager, standing on a ladder, was pouring champagne into the highest glass. Champagne glasses and champagne came raining down on her, soaking her wig and her dress.

"BITCH!" she spluttered, struggling to her feet. She snatched plastic mustard and ketchup bottles off the Sun King Burger Bar and flung herself at Mary, spraying her red and yellow before landing a sharp kick straight to her shin. Mary squealed and clutched her leg. Charles and her father stepped between the two women.

"Was that really necessary, Mary?" yelled Charles. "Honestly, I could cheerfully strangle you sometimes!"

"Stop all this at once!" Darell howled. "What the hell is going on here?"

A strand of Agatha's champagne-sodden wig flopped down over her nose before the whole top-heavy headpiece toppled forward and hit the floor with a splodge. She ripped off the hairnet that had held her own hair flat and ruffled it into some sort of shape with her hands.

"It's you," said Darell. "The Raisin woman!"

"I'm going to change." Mary sobbed, rushing off.

"I'd start with the chin if I was you," snarled Agatha, noting with satisfaction Mary's pronounced limp.

"That's quite enough, Agatha," said Charles. "Gustav, get some people to clean up that mess."

"And you lot!" shouted Darell, waving up at the orchestra. "You're being paid to play, so get on with it!"

The music restarted, the dancers returned to their partners and the party stuttered back to life. Charles led Agatha out of the ballroom, with Toni in tow.

"I'll call a taxi," said Toni, producing her phone. "Better reception outside. I'll . . . um . . . start walking down the drive to meet it."

Charles stood with Agatha on the steps outside the massive oak front door. Agatha could hear Toni muttering to herself as she walked away. "Don't go dousing yourself in champagne . . . drawing attention to yourself . . . Keep a low profile . . ."

"That didn't go entirely as I had hoped," she said, sitting down on the top step. Charles took a couple of steps down and leant against the stone wall.

"Far more entertaining than I thought it would be." He chuckled. "Mustard and ketchup? That was inspired."

"First things that came to hand," said Agatha forlornly. "What an embarrassment . . ."

"She hates mustard," said Charles.

Agatha's wig slipped out of her hand and tumbled down the steps like a soggy severed head.

"This may never recover." Charles laughed, stooping to pick it up. "But you will. Come on, I'll walk with you to meet that taxi."

Mary flung open her bedroom door and

marched into the large adjacent dressing room, ripping off her gown and kicking it across the floor. She pawed at the mustard splattered over her cheek. Agatha Raisin had gone too far this time! Too far! She would suffer for this. She felt tears welling in her eyes and went to wipe them away, then suddenly stopped. Mustard. Mustard in the eyes would be unbearable! How that woman would love her to miss out on the rest of the party with inflamed eyes. That was not going to happen. She would return to the party, laugh and smile and show everyone that a despicable old cow like Raisin could not get the better of her. She headed into her en suite bathroom to shower.

Minutes later, wrapped in a towel, she sat in front of the mirror at her dressing table, bathed in a pool of light, brushing her hair. She was considering what she should wear and how that would affect her choice of make-up when she suddenly had the chilling feeling that she was not alone.

"Hello, Darlinda," came a voice from the shadows. "You're missing the party."

Mary spun round and her eyes widened with terror.

"YOU!" she gasped. "What are you doing here? How did you get in?"

She leapt to her feet and dashed for the

bedroom door, only to find it locked. There was no way out.

Agatha and Charles walked slowly, at a pace dictated by Agatha's dress. They exchanged few words. They hadn't made it very far down the drive when Agatha stopped to fish a stone out of her shoe.

"I'm sorry," she said. "Not about Mary . . . I'm sorry that this is going to make things even worse for you."

"I can handle it," said Charles. "Don't worry about me, sweetie."

"But I do, Charles," Agatha said, "and there are things you're not telling me."

"Honestly, Aggie, I can't go into it all with you. I'm sworn to secrecy."

"I already know some of it," Agatha admitted. "The spa hotel plan, for instance."

Charles sighed and admitted that he was sorely troubled by that particular idea. Agatha knew that the taxi Toni had summoned would take an age to arrive, and with Charles all to herself, she continued to press him for details of his situation. She tried to come up with suggestions about how he could rid himself of the Brown-Fields, and their discussion ranged back and forth, Charles maintaining all the while that he was not at liberty to discuss the intricacies of his financial arrangements with his wife and in-laws.

"If they hear that I've let out even a whisper about —" He froze as a woman's scream cut through the stillness of the evening. It came again, and again — shrill, relentless, terrified.

"That's coming from the stable block," he said. "This way, hurry!"

Charles ran round the side of the house, past the door to the butler's pantry, with Agatha, having hitched up her skirts, hot on his heels. At the entrance to the stables they could see a young woman, sobbing hysterically, being comforted by a young man. The stable was brightly lit and Charles stopped in the doorway. Hanging by her neck from a wooden beam was Mary. She was wearing her riding clothes. Her eyes were closed and her head had been forced sideways by the large knot in the thick rope. Her arms were limp by her sides and her legs dangled neatly together.

"Quickly, Charles, there may still be time!" yelled Agatha, dashing past him.

She grabbed Mary's legs and lifted her, taking the weight off the rope. Charles swiftly righted a stepladder that was lying on its side and climbed up to loosen the rope around Mary's neck and undo it from the beam. It was clear when they laid the body gently on the stable floor, however, that their efforts were in vain.

Lady Mary Darlinda Fraith was dead.

CHAPTER FOUR

Other people arrived while Agatha and Charles were laying Mary's body on the floor of the stable. The security guards were first, followed by Gustav and a straggle of partygoers.

"Keep them all out of here, Charles," said Agatha. "Get Gustav to phone the police. Tell the security guards to make sure that no one leaves until the police get here, especially the couple who found the body."

Agatha looked down at Mary. The mustard-and-ketchup-stained gown was nowhere to be seen. She was dressed instead in her show-jumping outfit — black boots, white jodhpurs, a black jacket with a sparkling diamond horse brooch and a white shirt with a high collar. This is all utterly bizarre, thought Agatha. This is a classic suicide scene. Hanging is the most common form of suicide in the country, but none of this makes any sense. Why on earth did

Mary change into these clothes? And suicide? She was a strong-willed and very determined young woman. She certainly wasn't the sort to slope off and hang herself, even after the sort of confrontation we had on the dance floor. She was upset, but not suicidal. There is something very odd about all of this.

Agatha crouched over the body. The eyes were closed. On the eyelids, however, she noticed clusters of little red spots. There was also a swelling around the mouth and on closer inspection she could see that the lower lip was split, the small cut covered over with lipstick. I certainly didn't smack her in the mouth, she told herself, so how did that happen? And she hasn't done a very good job of covering it up.

She moved the rope slightly and noted the abrasion it had left on the neck. Then she spotted the edge of a bruise lower down and gently shifted the collar on the right side. There were a series of dark marks accompanied by small scratches. Finger marks, she concluded. Could I have done that when I grabbed her a few days ago? I didn't take much of a grip, so it hardly seems likely.

She pulled the collar at the other side to reveal another set of marks, then immediately stood up and backed away. She was startled by a piercing shriek followed by the sound of Linda Brown-Field screaming, "My baby! My baby! Charles, get that rope off her neck!" Tears were streaming down her face and Darell was at her side, supporting her as she wept and sobbed.

"Don't just stand there!" he yelled. "Do it, man!"

Charles turned towards the body but Agatha grabbed his arm, holding him back.

"You mustn't touch anything," she said. "She's been murdered."

"WHAT?!" Darell exploded. "Murdered? YOU did this!" He pointed an accusing finger at Charles. "YOU did this!"

"Don't be ridiculous!" Charles yelled. "I was nowhere near the —"

"Let's all try to calm down a little, shall we?" Detective Constable Alice Peterson hurried past the Brown-Fields into the barn and went straight to the body. With a radio crackling bursts of static, a female uni-formed police officer took up position just inside the doorway. Alice looked up at her colleague and shook her head. "No signs of life," she said softly.

"You got here quickly, Alice," Agatha said. The woman was the fiancée of Bill Wong, a detective sergeant she had known for many years.

"We were in the area," Alice explained. "Are you okay, Mrs. Raisin?"

"I'm fine," Agatha said, imagining the appalling effects a champagne shower and a sweaty sprint must have had on her make-up. "I must look a fright, but I'm all right."

"You're soaking wet," said Alice. "What happened here?"

The steady bright light of the stable was now punctuated by flickering blue, a police car having pulled up behind the house.

"A long story," said Agatha, "but this isn't suicide. I think she was murdered."

"Did you find the body?" asked Alice.

"No, the young couple over there did," Agatha explained, pointing. "Probably out here for nothing more sinister than a roll in the hay. We got her down but there was nothing we could do. She was dead."

"I see," said Alice. "Stay right here until the forensics people arrive, please."

"Well, well, Agatha Raisin." Chief Inspector Wilkes stood at the stable entrance. "At times like these, why is no one surprised to see you?"

"And everyone dismayed to see you," Agatha replied.

"I don't want any lip from you." Wilkes

114

scowled at her. "What's the situation, Peterson? Seems like a suicide."

"Things ain't always what they seem . . ." muttered Agatha, deep in thought.

"What?" snapped Wilkes. "What are you mumbling about, woman?"

"He murdered my daughter!" Darell shouted, pointing at Charles again. "Probably with help from her!" He jabbed the finger in Agatha's direction.

"Is that so?" A sly smile played on Wilkes's lips. Bill Wong appeared at his shoulder and exchanged a brief nod with Alice. "Keep them all here until forensics are finished with them, Sergeant," Wilkes said to Bill. "It's getting a little chilly. I'll be inside when we're ready to talk to them. Bound to be some tea and a spot of grub on the go."

Bill Wong led Agatha towards the library. She was wearing a paper forensic suit, the forensics officers having taken her clothes for examination, with a blanket wrapped around her shoulders. Toni wafted along beside them, still dressed in her pink gown.

"I'll hang around, Agatha," she said, "in case you need me."

"Thanks, Toni, but you'd best go home and get changed," said Agatha. "I'll call you if there's anything you can help with."

"I can have someone drive Toni home," Bill offered. "Listen to me, Agatha," he said, leaning in to speak quietly. The son of a Gloucestershire mother and a Hong Kong Chinese father, Bill was young, lean and handsome. He was one of the first people Agatha had come to know when she moved to Carsely and remained a trusted friend. "Wilkes wants to take your statement personally. You know what he's like. Don't wind him up. He's really gunning for you. Be careful."

"Thanks, Bill," said Agatha, giving him a smile, "but I have nothing to be frightened of."

Chief Inspector Wilkes was sitting at Charles's desk. Agatha was given a chair in front of the desk. Bill Wong stood to one side.

"What on earth have you got yourself mixed up in this time, Mrs. Raisin?" said Wilkes, grinning. "A very serious situation. Our pathologist has examined the body and is convinced that Lady Mary was cruelly murdered — strangled. The hanging scenario was simply a pathetically amateur attempt to cover up the murder. Now who do we know around here who is a pathetic amateur? What do you think, Sergeant Wong?"

"Mrs. Raisin tried to save the victim," said Bill.

"Unfortunately," said Agatha, "she was dead long before we got to her."

"And made a very good job of securing the crime scene," Bill added.

"All for show, though, wasn't it?" Wilkes sneered. "You were not invited to this party, were you, Mrs. Raisin? You even ended up starting a fight with the hostess — and she ended up dead."

"I wasn't the one who started —"

"And only a few days ago, you threatened to strangle her when you had another fight outside your own front door."

"How did you find out about that?"

"It's my job to find out about things like that, Mrs. Raisin. Care to comment about the front-door fight?"

"No, I thought I would just give you an ugly look, but you've already got one."

"Don't get smart with me. I know you threatened Lady Mary. You see, I am a police officer — a real detective — not some silly amateur woman playing at the job!"

"You couldn't detect a bear if it bit you in the arse!" Agatha snapped.

"Is that so?" growled Wilkes. "Well here's something I CAN do that you can't. Agatha Raisin, I am arresting you on suspicion of the murder of Lady Mary Fraith. You do not have to say anything, but it may harm your defence if you do not mention when questioned something which you later rely on in court. Anything you do say may be given in evidence. So — anything to say now, Mrs. Raisin?"

"Drop dead!"

"Take her and book her in at the station, Sergeant Wong. I look forward to having another little chat with you later, Mrs. Raisin."

Bill stepped forward and escorted Agatha towards the door.

"Wait a minute, Sergeant," called Wilkes. "Aren't you forgetting something?" He held his hands out in front of him, fists clenched, wrists together.

"Are you sure that's really necessary, sir?" objected Bill.

"Just do it!" ordered Wilkes. "This is a murder suspect."

Bill reached under his jacket and produced his handcuffs. "Sorry, Agatha," he whispered, clicking the cuffs over her wrists.

Wilkes smiled, gloating. His humiliation of Agatha Raisin was complete. Agatha glowered defiantly at him, holding her head high, assuming a calm dignity that even her baggy white paper overalls and devastated make-up could not suppress. "You're going to regret this," she said quietly.

Agatha was taken to Mircester police station. Bill Wong booked her in with the custody sergeant, who led her to a dull grey cell with a metal door. Bill's last words to her were "Don't worry, Agatha. You'll be out of here in no time." No time turned out to be six hours later, which included an hour of interrogation and accusation with the insufferable Wilkes. Eventually she was released without charge, as was Charles, who had undergone a similar ordeal. Toni and Gustav had arrived to take them home, bringing them fresh clothes. Bill Wong spoke to them both on the steps outside the police station.

"I really can't say very much," he told them, "but witnesses — partygoers and security staff — have given statements confirming your story. They saw you going off down the driveway. Toni and her taxi driver saw you running back towards the house. All the evidence we have points to the fact that you were in the wrong place at the wrong time to have been involved in Mary's murder. So you are off the hook — for now. Wilkes is still convinced that one or both of you are behind this."

"He's an idiot," said Agatha. "He doesn't know what he's talking about."

"He is dangerous," Bill said, "and he's going to use every means to dig up evidence against you."

"He won't find any," said Agatha, "because we didn't do it! In the meantime, the killer is somewhere out there free as a bird. We have to find who did it."

"Stay out of it, Agatha," Bill warned her. "As a friend, I don't want to see you getting hurt. You could find yourself in serious trouble if you get caught up in this investigation again."

"I know, Bill. I know that you're trying to give me good advice, and thank you for that — but I will get even with that cockroach Wilkes. Right now, I'm exhausted and I'm going home to bed."

Roy Silver arrived just after midday. Having spent most of the night either at Barfield House or in police custody answering endless versions of the same questions from Wilkes, Agatha had been out of bed for barely an hour when she opened the door to him. Roy stood there, suitcase in hand, ashen-faced.

"Aggie, darling!" he gushed. "I heard it all on the radio on the way here! Murder at

Barfield House! Unbelievable! You under arrest! You must be feeling — oh my God! What are you wearing?"

"It's a onesie, Roy," said Agatha. "Get over it."

Roy dropped his suitcase in the hall and followed Agatha through to the kitchen. She poured him a coffee and they sat at the table. Boswell and Hodge kept their distance from the stranger, eyeing him suspiciously before disappearing into the garden. Agatha related the events of the previous evening, Roy gasping and fanning his face at appropriate moments of high drama.

"So the mess that Charles was in just got even messier," she concluded.

"I'm afraid," said Roy, "that it may be even worse than you think."

"Worse?" Agatha groaned. "Come on, Roy, how could this possibly get any worse? What have you found out?"

"Well, obviously I have nothing in writing — no official documents or anything — but I've twisted a few arms, so to speak, and pieced together the deal that Charles did with the Brown-Fields. I've subsequently had one contact confirm that I've got it spot-on." He lifted his empty coffee cup and gave it a waggle.

"Help yourself," said Agatha. "Make some

fresh, but keep talking while you do."

"So we knew there was a financial arrangement attached to the marriage," said Roy, spooning coffee into a cafetière, "but this was far more than a simple marriage settlement. The Brown-Fields gave Charles a loan of two-point-seven-five million pounds . . ."

He paused for effect. Agatha let out a breath. It was way more than she had expected.

"But get this," he continued, "the loan was not to the estate, or to a company run by Charles, or to any sort of business set-up. It was a personal loan to Charles himself. His income from the estate has to be used to repay it, plus interest. A large chunk of the money went to clear his immediate debts, but he's not allowed to spend the rest any way he wants. He has to consult with the Brown-Fields and have them approve every major expenditure. If he falls behind in the repayments, or if the marriage falls apart, the loan and interest have to be repaid in full straight away.

"As his wife, Mary demanded that half the estate be signed over to her as part of the deal." Roy sat down with his coffee and consulted a small notebook. "Charles agreed because he apparently saw this as a way of him setting himself up for life. That's how they sold it to him — they persuaded him that all his money worries would be over, forever. He never expected to have them breathing down his neck night and day."

"He should have done," Agatha sighed. "He should have known better. He obviously thought he could charm the family, keep them happy and carry on as normal. The fool."

"Maybe not such a fool, Aggie," said Roy. "As his wife, and with half the estate already in her name, the rest of it would go to Mary if Charles died. He agreed to that only if, should she die — fall off one of her horses or whatever — all her property went to him."

"That's not so unusual," said Agatha, "for a married couple."

"But the Brown-Fields' problem is that, for tax reasons, one third of their entire fortune is in Mary's name. That all now goes to Charles — and it makes that loan they gave him look like a tiny little drop in the ocean."

"Surely they wouldn't have been so reckless? A riding accident could easily have done for her. Why would they take such a risk?"

"She was giving up competitive riding.

123

Apparently she wasn't going to have much time for it once she got her hands on Barfield House."

"Yes, I saw something of her plans," said Agatha showing Roy the document on her phone.

"Barfield House Luxury Hotel and Spa." Roy nodded. "I've seen a slightly different version of that document, darling. What you have is only the first page. The rest of it details schemes for developments of luxury homes on the Mircester and Carsely sides of the estate along with a golf course, a separate golf hotel and an equestrian centre."

"She would have torn the estate apart," said Agatha, "but now she's dead, and Charles stands to become an extremely wealthy man."

"The police will find all of this out sooner or later, Aggie," said Roy. "If Charles wasn't already their prime suspect, this will put him firmly in the frame."

"And that is just where old Darell wants him! That's why he was pointing the finger at Charles. If Charles is convicted, he'll be left with nothing. Darell will secure Mary's share of the Brown-Field millions and scoop up Barfield House and the estate into the bargain, while Charles rots in jail!"

They were interrupted by the ringing of telephone bells. Agatha grabbed her mobile phone. James had set that ringtone for her. The old-fashioned bells were a quaint gimmick, but she liked them. They served as a comforting reminder that this computer-camera-email-internetty gizmo was actually a telephone.

"Charles," she said, instantly recognising his voice. "We were just talking about you. How are you this morning?"

"I'm okay, sweetie," said Charles. "Terrible business. Terrible. Are you all right?"

"Apart from being accused of murder and spending half the night in a police cell, I'm fine."

"Good. Knew you would be. You're made of the right stuff, no doubt about it. That . . . well, that's why I need your help. Can you come over this afternoon?"

They arranged a time and Agatha dashed upstairs to change, leaving Roy in the kitchen with Boswell and Hodge, who had reappeared and were once again staring at him with feline mistrust. Roy didn't mind. He was going to Barfield House with Agatha Raisin, private detective, and was involved in a delicious murder investigation. So much better than watching the traffic in stuffy old London!

■ ■ ■ ■

Police officers were still milling around outside Barfield House when they arrived. The front door was open and Gustav met them as they walked inside.

"Have you met Roy Silver?" Agatha asked, introducing Roy.

"Pleased to meet you," said Roy, offering a hand, which Gustav pointedly ignored. "Isn't all of this simply awful?"

"If you say so," grumbled Gustav. "I'm still hoping it turns out more of a blessing in disguise, but that could take a bloody miracle now."

He showed them into the library, where Charles was waiting. They sat on the sofa while Charles took one of the wing-backed chairs, dispatching Gustav to fetch tea.

"That was one hell of a party last night," said Agatha. "I've never gone to a ball and left under arrest for murder before."

"And we're not out of the woods yet," said Charles. "I have been assured in no uncertain terms that I am still the prime suspect. I can't say too much, but Mary's father —"

"Charles," Agatha butted in. "Roy and I know all about the contract with the Brown-Fields and the plans for the luxury homes, the golf club — everything."

"How did you . . . ?"

"I'm a detective," said Agatha, "and Roy is very good at ferreting out information."

"Good . . ." said Charles, then paused as Gustav came in with a tea tray.

"Tea," grunted the butler.

"That will be all, Gustav," said Charles.

"What, no cake with a hacksaw baked inside for you to saw through your prison bars?"

Charles waved him away.

"Tell no one about the financial arrangements," he said. "There is a non-disclosure clause in the contract, and if the Brown-Fields suspect I have been talking to you about it, I'm done for."

"My team will have to know," said Agatha, "otherwise they could come across evidence without realising its significance."

"Very well," said Charles, "but they are not to talk about it to any outsiders."

"Mum's the word," said Roy. He made a zipping motion across his mouth, turned an imaginary key in a lock and threw the key away. Charles gave him a look of grave concern.

"Are you sure he's going to be . . . ?"

"He'll be fine," said Agatha. "What do you want me to do?"

127

"I want you to investigate the murder," said Charles. "Mary's father appears to be well connected with ranking police officers — that Wilkes chap and his superiors. You know what these people are like — Masonic lodges, golf clubs . . ."

"Golf clubs," said Agatha. "And the Brown-Fields were planning to build one."

"That would have been Darell's vanity project," said Charles. "My understanding is that golf clubs are closing down all over the country these days. No money to be made in that business. He was obsessed with the game, though. In any case, he'll do everything he can to make sure that I'm the one who carries the can for Mary's murder. I need you to find the real culprit and prove me innocent. It seems that Mary made enemies wherever she went. She was very good at antagonising people. I should think there will be no shortage of suspects for her murder."

"I've been marked as a suspect too," Agatha reasoned. "Wilkes will try to block me at every turn. He hates me. I won't be able to use any of our police contacts. It will be tough."

"I have no doubt it will. I will pay you double your normal rate — whatever it takes for you and your team to get to the bottom of this."

"I'm already involved, Charles. You know I would be looking into this anyway, so money really isn't a problem."

"Money certainly won't be a problem if you can prove me innocent," said Charles, "but you will be paid on performance. A fat fee if you find the real murderer, but nothing at all if I'm found guilty — I won't have a penny left to pay you with."

"Well, I guess we start with her show-jumping cronies," said Agatha. "Dressing her up in that outfit has to mean something. Do you know any of that lot?"

"Here's the guest list from the party." Charles handed her a sheet of paper. "I don't know too many of her friends, but the ones I know are involved with the horses are highlighted. I understand there's a special charity event in two days' time at Mircester Manor Park. They're all bound to be there."

"Then we shall be there too," said Agatha, getting to her feet. "Come on, Roy. There's a lot of work to do."

Agatha called her team together in the Raisin Investigations offices early the following morning. They all crowded around her desk and Helen provided tea. Simon placed a plate of beautifully baked tarts in the middle of the desk.

"What are these?" Agatha asked. "They look good enough for the Carsely Ladies' Society Bake Off."

"From a grateful client," Simon explained. "Home-baked rhubarb tarts from Mrs. Fletcher as a thank you for sorting out her problem."

"Well done," Agatha congratulated him as everyone helped themselves to a tart. "You go first then. I want to get up to date with everything before I brief you on our biggest ever case. You all know Roy," she added, waving her tart in his direction. "He's going to be helping us out. So, Simon — tell us about the phantom pooper."

Simon slid a thick folder across the desk.

"It's all in my report," he said, "but I can give you a summary. Basically, it was her husband. I caught him making a deposit — caught him with his trousers down, so to speak. I really surprised him when the camera flash went off. If he hadn't already been doing it, he would have sh—"

"Photos — really?" Agatha wrinkled her nose.

"They're in the file. He put the excrement through two different treatments to remove all pathogens," said Simon, "and then used it as fertiliser. He said it brought his rhubarb on a treat."

Everyone stared at their half-eaten rhubarb tarts. Simon burst out laughing.

"It's perfectly safe," he said, "but Mr. Fletcher didn't think his wife would like his little experiment, so he didn't tell her. She knows now, obviously."

"Okay, Simon," said Agatha, dropping the remnants of her tart into the bin and taking a big gulp of tea. "Good work. Patrick, what about the Philpott case?"

"In brief," said Patrick, handing over his report, "Philpott's new MD is an impostor. The real Harold Cheeseman is still in Australia. The impostor is a cleaner who worked at Cheeseman's previous firm. He rifled through the personnel files, came across Cheeseman's photo and CV, realised that they looked quite alike and conned his way into the top job with Philpott. We need to advise Philpott to have him arrested for fraud."

"Take care of that, would you, Patrick?" said Agatha.

They quickly ran through the other cases on the books, including the Chadwick divorce case, before Agatha pulled an envelope from her drawer and began to arrange some photos on the desk.

"We have been engaged by Sir Charles Fraith," she said, slapping down his photo, "to investigate the murder of his wife, the former Mary Darlinda Brown-Field."

Agatha explained everything that had happened leading up to the murder and Roy filled them in on the financial situation between Charles and the Brown-Fields. He stressed the need for secrecy.

"The police will find out all about it," said Patrick, "and your sources already know, Roy. It's not going to be any kind of secret for very much longer."

"We need to make sure that we're not the ones spreading it around," said Agatha. "Apart from anything else, it gives Charles a compelling motive for the murder. We don't want to reinforce the idea that he did it for the money and to save his estate."

"So who else is a potential suspect?" Simon asked.

"Well, there's me," said Agatha, putting her own photograph on the table. "I am widely known to have despised the victim and to have come to blows with her. Some would say this was out of jealousy because she married the man I was in love with . . ."

She took a breath, looking around the

room into the eyes of each of her team in turn.

". . . but that is absolute rubbish. I am not a murderer. I did not kill Mary. She was a hateful character and I wanted Charles out of her clutches, but for his sake, not mine. Given time, I would have found a way. Murder would not have been my way."

"We all know it wasn't you," Toni said. "Who else has a motive for murder?"

"Gustav." Agatha placed his photograph on the desk. "He works for Charles and hates the Brown-Fields, especially Mary. He believed that she was going to have him sacked. He is also intensely loyal to Charles and suspected that Mary was going to destroy his family heritage.

"Mrs. Tassy." She produced another photo. "Charles's aunt. She detests the Brown-Fields and rarely leaves her room now that they are in residence at Barfield. An unlikely suspect, especially given the circumstances of the murder — she's not physically strong enough to have overpowered Mary and strung her up — but we need to keep an open mind."

"She and Gustav could have been working together," Simon suggested.

"That's possible," Agatha agreed, "and in keeping an open mind, we should consider that. Wilkes certainly will. He may even believe that we were all in it together, but he is wrong as usual. The murderer isn't in these photos. The riding gear indicates that this is someone who crossed swords with Mary on the show-jumping circuit."

"Or that could be a complete red herring," said Patrick, "to direct attention away from everyone in our photos here."

"Maybe," said Agatha, "but I still think the riding outfit is significant. It takes a peculiarly sick mind to dress someone you've just murdered — all the while risking someone discovering you in the act — and then stage a suicide. That all has to mean something."

"According to Charles," said Toni, "Mary was not well liked, so why were there so many people at her party?"

"Who wants to miss a good party?" Roy volunteered. "We know that a lot of the Brown-Fields' so-called friends were business associates who would use a function like that for networking, but in the kind of social set Mary was mixing with, a party like this would be an event to be seen at. Nobody would want to be left out."

"We need to find out a lot more about Mary and that set," said Agatha. "In the meantime, we all have to be wary of these two. They desperately want to pin the murder on Charles, probably with me as his accomplice." She laid photographs of Darell and Linda Brown-Field on the desk.

"Wait a minute!" said Simon. "That's him!"

"That's who?" Agatha asked.

"There's no mistaking that chin now that I see it again," Simon said, picking up Darell's photograph. "That's the bloke who's been seeing Mrs. Chadwick at that house in Oxford!"

"But she called out to George," said Toni. "She shouted for George to fetch the shotgun."

"There was no George," Agatha began to smile, "and there was no shotgun. They were having a damned good laugh at our expense. She didn't know it was us out there, of course. She just shouted to scare off anyone who might be hanging around and then they both had a giggle about it!"

"So Darell Brown-Field is having an affair with Sheraton Chadwick," said Simon. "Though we've still no photo to confirm that for Mr. Chadwick."

"Let's keep it to ourselves for the time being," Agatha decided. "The murder investigation has to take priority and it could be useful to have that little titbit of information about Darell. No mention of this to Mr. Chadwick until we see how it all fits together and — Toni!" A sudden realisation dawned. "The horse brooch that was on Mary's jacket! Mrs. Chadwick has one exactly like it!"

"That was a very expensive-looking item," said Toni. "Gold and diamonds. The kind of gift a rich man might buy. A rich man like Darell?"

"Really?" said Patrick, scowling and shaking his head. "He'll have done a deal, I bet. Bargained for a hefty discount for buying two — one for his daughter and one for his mistress. Unbelievable."

"Patrick," Agatha said, "I want you to dig up everything you can on the Brown-Fields, especially Darell. He's a golfer. See what you can find out about that. And see if there's anything more we can find out about Gustav as well. His past is still something of a mystery."

Patrick nodded. Out of the corner of her eye, Agatha could see Roy clutching his hands together with excitement. He was beside himself at the thought of being part of a murder investigation. So he should be, Agatha thought. This is exciting stuff!

"Simon," she said, "I want you back on the Chadwick case. Mrs. Chadwick is tied into this now. Keep up the surveillance and keep trying for a photograph of Darell coming or going. I will get Charles to send us a photo of Mary wearing that brooch. Track down where it was bought or the jeweller who made it.

"Toni and Roy, we need to start researching the show-jumping business. We're going to an event tomorrow and we need to have some idea of what we're looking at when we get there. We also need to find out more about these people before we go, so that we know who we're talking to." She gave the two of them a copy of the party guest list with Mary's riding friends highlighted.

"Okay, everyone, let's get on with it — we have a murderer to find!"

Mircester Manor Park lay on the opposite side of town from Charles's estate. The stone wall surrounding it ran along a grass verge, with a ditch separating it from the main road. On the other side of the road was a large housing estate, giving the impression that the area was heavily built up, but that all changed when Toni drove through the stone arched gateway into Manor Park. Agatha guessed that the arch was high enough and wide enough to accommodate two horse-drawn carriages passing beneath it, as it would have to have done when it was originally built. A weather-ravaged, barely discernible coat of arms was carved on the keystone of the arch.

Beyond the arch was flat open parkland. Unlike the approach to Barfield House, there was no avenue of trees leading up to a grand residence. Instead, a few specimen trees were dotted here and there, with more dense woodland lying beyond the acres of open grass. The road swept into the far distance, where an intriguing Palladian mansion stood proudly on a low rise. The house was framed by the woodland behind it. Above, the wide expanse of blue sky, scrubbed by occasional slow-moving clouds, appeared infinitely vast.

The areas of interest for Agatha, Toni and Roy, however, were the oceans of lawn either side of the road. Tents, pavilions and market stalls were scattered around fenced-off areas where showground arenas had been created. The one to the left was flat and empty apart from a female rider sitting tall in the saddle trotting across it on a glossy chestnut pony. The arena to the right was laid out with a series of colourful gates and jumps. Agatha consulted an event map that Toni had printed out from the Manor Park website.

"That's obviously the show-jumping arena," she said, pointing to the right, "and on the other side is the dressage enclosure. We should be able to park farther up on the left."

The car park was busy, with very few spaces left, and Agatha was impressed at how well attended the charity event was, given that it was midweek. She scanned the crowds of people milling around the various stalls selling snacks, souvenirs and all manner of equestrian equipment and ephemera. Toni and Roy stood either side of her, studying the map. Roy was wearing brown brogues, corduroy trousers, a checked tweed jacket, contrasting checked shirt and a flat cap — every town-dweller's idea of how a gentleman dressed in the countryside. Toni was in a waxed jacket, jeans and boots. Unlike Roy, she would blend into the crowd and go almost unnoticed. Agatha had chosen a sober grey trouser suit and black shoes with wedge heels, having long ago discovered that any high heels other than wedges spiked themselves into soft ground with a wanton, ankle-twisting disregard for a girl's dignity.

"We need to split up," she said. "Concentrate on those areas where the horse boxes are. Ask around for the people on our party guest list and try to engage any of the competitors in conversation. We need to find out as much as we can about what Mary got up to at these events and who might have a grudge against her. We need a list of her enemies."

Roy set off eagerly to play detective. Toni sniffed the air, winced and coughed. The heady scent of horse was everywhere.

"Does that smell remind you of anything?" she asked Agatha.

"If you mean burying myself in a pile of straw and donkey shit not too long ago to hide from a maniac who was trying to put a bullet in my head," said Agatha, "not at all. The thought never entered my mind."

Toni laughed. "I'm glad you can see the funny side of it now."

"Ruined one of my favourite outfits," Agatha smiled. "All right, I'm going this way — you try over there."

Agatha approached a group of half a dozen young women standing chatting by a cluster of horse boxes. Their ages seemed to range from mid twenties to mid thirties. They were all of similar build — slim and athletic — with their hair tied back in ponytails. All wore white jodhpurs and black boots. Their jackets, she decided, were the only things that stopped them from looking like identical clones. Unlike Mary and Mrs. Chadwick, they were not all dressed in black jackets. Some wore royal blue, one a luxurious dark green and another deep purple. A couple of them were smoking cigarettes.

"Excuse me," said Agatha. "Can you help me? I'm looking for —"

"And you are?" said one of the smokers, turning and blowing a grey cloud at her. That, Agatha knew, was designed to tell someone they weren't welcome, to make them feel they were regarded as inferior and generally to piss them off. She knew because she'd done it herself more times than she could remember. She refused to be intimidated.

"I know who she is," said another of the women. "She's that detective — Sally Sultana or something."

"Agatha Raisin," said Agatha, forcing a polite smile. "I'd like to talk to you about —"

"Well we don't want to talk to you," said the smoker, turning her back.

"I quite understand," Agatha said, as the women resumed their conversation. "Sorry to have bothered you." Then she tapped the smoker lightly on the shoulder and whispered in her ear, "There's a really horrible muddy mark on the back of your trousers.

Makes it look like you've . . . you know . . . had a bit of an accident."

She walked off, looking back after a few paces to see the smoker, having discreetly separated from her friends, contorting herself by the wing mirror of a Range Rover trying to find a muddy mark that simply wasn't there.

After several more fruitless attempts to talk to women who were either too uninterested or too busy to spare her even a few seconds, Agatha met up with Roy and Toni.

"I can't believe this lot," said Toni. "Nobody's prepared to say a word about Mary."

"They're talking about her amongst themselves," said Roy. "I've heard them giggling like schoolgirls when her name is mentioned, but they won't speak to me."

"I think they've been warned off," said Agatha. "I feel the hand of Darell Brown-Field in this. Come on, let's find somewhere we can sit down and have a drink."

They made for a refreshment stand, in front of which a herd of plastic tables and chairs was corralled. A familiar voice rang out from behind the counter.

"Hello there, Mrs. Raisin! Fancy seeing you here!"

"Doris," said Agatha, happy to encounter the friendly face of Doris Simpson, her faithful cleaning lady. "I didn't expect to see you here either."

"My cousin Rita's girl Zoe asked me to help out," said Doris, indicating a young woman wiping down the tables. "Well, it's for charity, isn't it? You enjoying an afternoon off?"

"Not really," Agatha admitted. "We're here on business. We had hoped to talk to some of the riders, but they're not very communicative."

"If you mean they're a bunch of snooty cows, I completely agree," said Doris. "Zoe — do you know anybody Mrs. Raisin could talk to about the horsey contest things? Folks here have been giving her the cold shoulder."

"Not surprised about that," Zoe said, wringing out her cloth. "Them that's here today is the worst lot of snobs around. Ain't seen none of the nice ones here. You should try talking to Tamara Montgomery, though. She's the best. She runs the Montgomery Stables over by Blockley."

"Would she have known Mary Brown-Field — the woman who was murdered?" asked Toni.

"Oh, she knew that one all right. Hated her, she did. I seen her in tears more than once after a run-in with Mary."

143

"Really?" Agatha said. "Is Tamara here today?"

"Not today. She don't compete no more. Still has her stables, though."

"I think we need to talk to Tamara," said Agatha, pushing a ten-pound note into the charity box on the counter. "Thank you for your help."

"Not at all," Doris smiled. "I'll do you Monday as usual. Bye!"

"Finally," said Toni, starting the car, "a lead to someone we can assume was one of Mary's enemies."

"I'd have thought the list of her enemies would have been as long as my arm," said Roy.

"I bet it's as long as both your arms, Roy," Agatha agreed, "but somebody doesn't want us meeting the people on that list."

"Daddy Darell," said Toni.

"Without a doubt," Agatha nodded, "but he's not keeping people quiet on his own. Somebody's helping him out. Maybe we'll find out more when we talk to Tamara Montgomery."

"You want to go to Blockley now?" asked Toni.

"No, it's getting late," said Agatha, "and

I'm famished. I think an early dinner is in order."

"The Red Lion?" Roy suggested.

"Good idea," Agatha grinned. "Red Lion tonight. Tamara tomorrow!"

CHAPTER FIVE

The following morning, with Toni in the office catching up on some paperwork, Agatha and Roy set off to pay a visit to the Montgomery Stables. Roy had offered to drive, but Agatha found his sparkling gold Lexus a little ostentatious for her taste and far too conspicuous for a private detective, so they took her anonymous dark-grey saloon instead.

"You certainly brighten up the inside of this car," she said, eyeing Roy's burgundy chinos, yellow waistcoat and dusky pink shirt. Agatha loved colourful fashion, providing that colour was deployed with taste and elegance. For business, muted colours were often more appropriate. Her own light-grey skirt and jacket almost matched the car's upholstery.

"It's called style, darling," Roy smiled, waving a hand in a sweeping theatrical gesture. "Don't even attempt to understand."

Agatha sighed, shook her head and started the engine.

The stables were tucked away amid a patchwork of fields beyond Blockley on the road to Draycott. They approached the cluster of stable buildings along a track with a copse of oak trees to one side and a four-bar wooden fence to the other. The fence enclosed a flat area surfaced with what looked to Agatha like a mixture of ash and rags. From her research, she knew this was a special material spread on areas used for training horses. Beyond this enclosure was an old farmhouse and a structure that looked like a small barn. Another enclosure near the barn was laid out with show-jumping gates and walls. Three horses grazed in a paddock adjacent to the show-jumping area.

As they pulled up outside the farmhouse, they were greeted by a pleasant, rosy-cheeked woman in her late thirties wearing a heavy sweater, beige jodhpurs and muddy boots. A black Labrador dashed from her side and danced around Agatha and Roy, lashing their legs with his tail in a lavish welcome ritual.

"Piper, here!" called the woman and the

dog slunk back to her side. "Sorry about that. He loves visitors. Can I help you?" she asked, wiping her hands on a towel.

"We're looking for Tamara Montgomery," said Agatha, frowning at Piper's muddy paw mark on top of her sandal.

"You've found her." Tamara smiled, and Agatha noted the lines that appeared at the sides of her mouth, as well as the crinkles at the corners of her eyes. This woman wore no make-up. "What can I do for you?"

Agatha introduced herself and Roy, explaining that they needed to talk to her about Mary Brown-Field. Tamara's face fell.

"I can't help you," she said.

"We know that you and Mary had . . . issues," said Agatha. "We're trying to find out more about her. Her father has accused Sir Charles Fraith of murdering her. We need to make sure that he can't railroad the murder investigation. Sir Charles didn't do it. We have to make that clear or the Brown-Fields will crush him."

"I don't know . . ." Tamara said, shaking her head. Agatha had noticed her shoulders droop slightly when the Brown-Fields were mentioned, almost as if the mere thought of them had drained a little life from her. "You'd better come inside."

She showed them into the main farmhouse

building, pausing in the porch to remove her boots. Piper trotted ahead of her. A wide door with upper panels that were a delicate web of stained-glass flowers led into the hall. Piper nudged it open with his head. Tamara turned right to take them into the kitchen. Agatha glanced left, where there was a neat office with a desk, computer and filing cabinets. The kitchen was tidy and clean. Tamara offered them coffee and they sat at wooden chairs around a long table. Under the table, Agatha felt the soft, warm body of Piper as he draped himself across her feet. The silvery grey sandals she was wearing left most of her feet exposed. A heavy Labrador blanket might be nice on a cold winter morning, she thought, but it wouldn't take long today for her feet to overheat. She gave the dog a nudge with her toes. He was way heavier than Boswell or Hodge and refused to budge.

"I'm sorry about what happened to Mary," Tamara said.

"I would agree with you," Agatha replied, "but then we'd both be lying wouldn't we?"

Tamara stared at her, clearly taken aback; possibly, thought Agatha, even slightly appalled that she had been so forthright.

"Don't look so shocked," she said. "I wouldn't have wished what happened to

Mary on anyone, but I won't pretend that I'm sad she's gone. I had plenty of reasons to hate her, and I've heard that you did too."

Tamara opened her mouth as if to respond, then burst into tears, burying her face in her hands. She pushed back her chair, the legs screeching as they scraped across the tiled kitchen floor, stood up to grab a handful of kitchen roll and blew her nose loudly. Piper scuttled out from beneath the table and made for the safety of his basket in the corner of the room. Agatha wiggled her toes to cool off her feet.

"It's true," Tamara gasped, wiping her eyes and sucking in great gulps of air. "I had . . . no . . . reason to like Mary or her family."

"It seems that they're not easy people to like," said Roy. "Believe me, Tamara, you are not alone."

"You don't understand," said Tamara, calming herself and taking her seat again. "They made my life a living hell. They are utterly despicable," she added, a note of anger in her voice, "and I hate the whole bloody lot of them!"

"Again," said Agatha, "you're not alone."

"But I didn't kill her," Tamara said quickly. "I could never do anything like that."

"Somebody killed her," Agatha said. "The

police even think that I may have had a hand in it. I didn't, but there's no doubt that I had a motive. What had Mary done to make you despise her? What might give *you* a motive?"

"I don't think I can . . ."

"Have you already been interviewed by the police?" Roy asked.

"No, no, they haven't . . ."

"They will," said Agatha. "Eventually they will come to speak to you and you will have to tell them the truth. Whatever was between you and Mary will come out — unless I can find the murderer first and hand him, or her, to the police on a plate. Anything you can tell us might help with that."

"It's all to do with this place," Tamara sighed. "The stables. My mother died two years ago and my father followed soon after. They left this house and the stables to me, along with a fair amount of cash. I was still competing then — I've been riding since before I could walk — but I never truly re-alised how much it all cost. My parents must have spent a fortune over the years to get me to the level I was at. With them gone, I had to cope on my own, and the business here began to suffer."

"But everything around here looks in such good order," said Roy. "Even outside is neat and clean. At a stables, I expected a lot more mud and . . . other stuff."

"I work hard to keep everything ship-shape," said Tamara, "and I get a little help from a couple of local girls who do chores in return for riding lessons, and a friend who helps out from time to time. The real problem is that I have no clients."

"What do you mean?" Agatha asked. "And what's this got to do with the Brown-Fields?"

"When money started getting tight," Tamara explained, "I suppose people must have realised that I was struggling. I had some small local sponsors, but it was never enough. Then I was approached at an event by a man who offered me a tempting amount of money to make sure that I didn't win. He said it was a betting scam. I was desperate. I took the money."

"Was this man Mary's father?" Roy asked.

"No, no, he would never get involved in anything like that personally," Tamara explained, "but it must have been someone who worked for them. So I threw the contest — like a boxer taking a dive in the fourth round. It was some time later that Mary came to me at another event and showed me photographs — photographs of me accepting a wad of cash from that man. She said she would expose me as a cheat unless I helped her to win and kept myself out of the running."

"Blackmail!" said Roy. "She was a cunning little devil, wasn't she?"

"But you couldn't actually guarantee her any wins could you?" Agatha reasoned. "There were lots of other talented riders competing. She couldn't get to them all, so why risk blackmailing you?"

"Because she and her father had something else in mind," said Tamara. "When I stopped winning, appeared to lose my form, my sponsors had to withdraw their funding. Then rumours started spreading that I was all at sea without my parents. People used to pay a lot for stabling here. But they love their horses — I completely understand that — and who would risk an animal they loved with a woman they had heard might be losing her marbles?

"One by one they drifted away, until now the only horses left here are my own. The Brown-Fields were behind those rumours, I'm sure of that. Mary offered to buy the business. She offered less than half what it's worth. She was furious when I wouldn't sell it to her, but I couldn't just sell up and go — this is my home! She kept on at me, threatening, bullying, telling me and everyone else how useless I was and that the business was a mess. Now I suppose her father will start coming after me . . ."

"They had plans for their own equestrian centre," said Agatha. "Maybe they saw you as competition and wanted you out of the way. That would be just like Mary."

"And she may well get what she wants, even from beyond the grave," Tamara admitted, shaking her head. "When you arrived I thought for a second that you might be new clients, but . . ."

"Buck up!" said Agatha cheerily, the germ of an idea forming in her head. "You need to find your old competitive spirit again, Tamara. You might be down now, but you're not out. You're still standing and you mustn't give up. We never give up, do we, Roy?"

"Never," agreed Roy. "You don't allow it."

"And I'm not allowing it now, either." Agatha nodded. "Come on, Tamara, why don't you show us around?"

"All right," said Tamara, giving herself a shake. "Let's go outside."

Piper leapt out of his basket, wagging his tail, and led the way back to the front door. Tamara pointed out the exercise area that Agatha and Roy had passed as they drove in, showed them the food store, the stable yard, the loose boxes and the tack room, where saddles, reins, blankets and all manner of riding paraphernalia were stowed neatly on shelves. It all, thought Agatha, looks delightfully fresh and inviting, if you're a horse.

"The rear of the barn," said Tamara, pointing, "is a traditional hay store, but the front has been converted into a spa area."

"Sounds lovely," said Agatha. "Relaxing in a hot tub after being bounced around in a saddle must be very soothing for your . . . bottom."

"It's not for the riders," laughed Tamara. "It's for the horses!"

She flung open a side door to the barn and they walked into a space that was taken up mainly by a long, narrow pool and a fibreglass-and-steel contraption that looked big enough to contain a large horse.

"Quite narrow for swimming laps, I'd have thought," said Roy, nodding at the pool.

"It's not really for swimming," Tamara explained. "We can make water flow down the pool at varying rates, and the horse walks against the flow. Over there," she said, pointing to the contraption, "is a kind of jacuzzi. The aqua therapies help to deal with any niggling little injuries the horses might pick up."

Leaving the barn, they strolled in the sunshine down to the paddock, where the three horses walked over to join them at the fence. The largest of the three was a glossy chestnut with a white blaze down the middle of its face. The other two were roughly equal in size, one grey and one black. The chestnut nuzzled Roy's shoulder and he stroked its nose. From somewhere inside her sweater Tamara produced an apple. Holding it in both hands, she squeezed, twisted and broke it in half. Agatha was impressed. Tamara was a strong woman. Had she and Mary ever gone head to head, Tamara would certainly have come out on top.

"That's Saturn," Tamara said to Roy, handing him half the apple. "You can give him this. Hold it in the flat of your hand. He's very gentle."

"He's magnificent," said Roy. Agatha was a little surprised at the way Roy was gazing at Saturn. The horses had the same sort of soft, adorable eyes as Wizz-Wazz, the donkey they had both come to know not too long ago, but they were far bigger creatures. In fact, up close, they were so big that Agatha decided to keep her distance.

"The police will ask," she said, declining a proffered piece of apple to feed one of the other horses, "where you were on Saturday when Mary was murdered."

"I was here," said Tamara. "One of the girls was here with me until her parents came to pick her up."

"And who are these two beauties?" Roy asked stroking the other horses. Agatha frowned at him. They had come here to question Tamara, but that was not the sort of question they needed to be asking. They were supposed to be investigating a murder, not patting ponies!

"Cloud and Midnight," said Tamara. "You can probably guess which is which."

"Do you know anyone else we might talk to who held a grudge against Mary?"

"There was one French girl — Claudette, I never knew her second name — who couldn't stand her," said Tamara. "I believe they actually came to blows. That was a real surprise because Claudette was such a lovely person. Then, of course, there was Deborah Lexington. That was a huge tragedy. It was all glossed over as an accident, but Deborah has never recovered. She can't ride any more. Can't even walk, from what I heard."

"Really?" said Agatha. "I think we need to talk to both of them. Do you have their details?"

"I do for Deborah, I think."

"Was she a friend of yours?"

"I wouldn't say that. Her horses were beautiful and she made sure they were very well looked after, but I think she liked the idea of being associated with the sport more than the horses themselves. Her family had lots of money and she was keen that everyone knew it. She used to spray very expensive perfume around. She said she adored horses but didn't want to smell like one. She and her brother live not too far away, but if you want to talk to Claudette, you had best contact the Colonel."

"The Colonel?" Roy arched an eyebrow. "Sounds very mysterious."

"Not at all," Tamara smiled, running her hand down Midnight's neck and pressing her face to the side of his head, something the horse obviously loved. That, thought Agatha, is clearly why she doesn't invest in make-up. "The Colonel is one of the good guys. He's involved in organising the events, the scoring and the overall rankings of the competitors. He must be nearly eighty now but he's still very much on the ball. He knows everyone. He will definitely know Claudette."

"Would he have been at the charity event at Mircester Manor Park?" Agatha asked.

"I doubt it," Tamara said. "That wasn't

part of the competition calendar. The top riders wouldn't have been there either. They would have been in France, preparing for the event in Bordeaux this weekend. They like to have as much time as possible to settle their horses and get them in shape after they've been transported any great distance."

"Can you put us in touch with the Colonel?"

"Of course. We can phone him from my office."

"Thank you," Agatha said as they began to walk back towards the farmhouse. "You've been a big help. In return, we may be able to do something for you."

"We may?" said Roy.

"Yes," said Agatha, "and it's more of a 'you' than a 'we.' You see, Tamara, Roy is something of a public relations and marketing genius. He is the man behind Wizz-Wazz the donkey."

"I thought I recognised you!" said Tamara, turning to Agatha, realisation dawning on her face. "You're the Donkey Lady, the one who was on TV saying 'Snakes and b—' "

"That's entirely beside the point," Agatha butted in, skating over the brief moment of celebrity that had been generated by her infamous TV appearance with the flatulent

Wizz-Wazz. "Roy is just the man to put your stables on the map."

"I am?" said Roy.

"You are," Agatha assured him. "You have all the right contacts to bring in sponsorship, and with Tamara's help you'll be able to reach out to everyone who should know about this fantastic facility. A fresh image, some marketing spin and you can give Montgomery Stables a real shot in the arm."

"Well, I suppose I could," said Roy, stroking his chin.

"But . . . but there's no way I can pay for that sort of help," said Tamara.

"We could start off," said Roy, gazing towards the horses in the paddock, "with a few riding lessons in lieu of a fee, then work something out once things are up and running again."

"That would be marvellous," said Tamara. "Mrs. Raisin, I don't know how I can ever thank you . . ."

"Just make it work," said Agatha. "With Roy's help, you have to turn this place into a huge success. That will be a real poke in the eye for the Brown-Fields."

In the office, Tamara called the Colonel and introduced Agatha, who arranged to pay him a visit that afternoon. Once Tamara had dug out Deborah Lexington's address,

Agatha and Roy said their goodbyes, Piper escorting them to the car before galloping back when Tamara called him.

"That was a great idea, Aggie," said Roy, buckling his seat belt. "I never thought about learning to ride before, but I know I'm going to love it. Saturn is just gorgeous, isn't he? I'll have to get all the gear, of course — the boots, those trousery things, the black hat . . ."

"I want you to keep an eye on Tamara," said Agatha. "She seems perfectly nice, but she had plenty of reason to want Mary dead. She is also clearly a great source of information about Mary's friends and enemies. I need you back here to start working with her tomorrow and finding out all you can."

"Find out all . . . Oh my God!" Roy gasped, holding a hand to his chest. "I'm going under cover!"

Roy babbled with excitement all the way back to Mircester. He was going to learn to ride, he was investigating a murder and he was to be working on a covert operation. He was practically a secret agent! Agatha was relieved to be able to drop him off in Mircester at an upmarket department store where she knew they would be delighted to sell him the finest equestrian clothing at eye-watering prices. She realised that she would have to suffer a mini fashion parade when she got home later, but it would be worth it to have some peace and quiet while she found her way to the Colonel's house. She put in a quick call to Toni to ask her to dig up some background on Deborah Lexington, then set off.

Colonel Steven Warbler-Dow lived in Maugersbury, just outside Stow-on-the-Wold. Agatha had been given specific directions about how to reach the house, but more than once had the feeling that she must have gone wrong. The roads were so narrow and flanked so tightly in places by enviably opulent family homes that she felt as if she must be on a driveway, passing through the carefully tended gardens. Where houses gave way to hedgerows, she caught glimpses of glorious countryside, folds of green rolling into distant hills bathed in sunshine.

Before long, she identified a turning that took her to the short stone-chip driveway of the Colonel's house. To the right was a lawn, separated from the drive by a flower bed bursting with spring colour. Ahead was the house itself, a large two-storey L-shaped villa with an elaborate thatched roof that made Agatha's own look positively primitive. Along the ridge line the thatch was doubly thick, the edges cut in a traditional skirt of curves and points, before it swooped down, curving gracefully around upstairs windows that peeked out from beneath the grey reeds. Where part of the ground floor extended out beyond the upper wall line, the thatch cascaded lower still, the angle of the roof allowing it to cover the extension. It was a delightful house, large enough, Agatha guessed, to swallow both her cottage and James's, but small enough still to be a very comfortable home.

She parked close to the house, beside a wooden garage that she estimated could house at least three cars, and stepped out to be greeted by a loud "Hello, there!" from an elderly man striding confidently towards her. He was tall, with a grey beard and a balding head, a combination that Agatha had never found particularly attractive, although his beaming smile and twinkling blue eyes more than compensated for him having hair growing in the wrong places. You must have been a handsome devil in your youth, she thought, and you haven't lost it entirely.

"You must be Agatha," he said.

"And you are the Colonel?" she responded, shaking his hand.

"Steven, please," he said. "Come inside. Can't talk in this scorching sun."

They walked towards the house, past a tangled heap of rusting metal that Agatha had first taken to be a sculpture but now realised was an old lawnmower.

"What happened to your mower?" she asked.

"Damn thing was always breaking down," explained the Colonel, chuckling. "So I shot the bugger. Put it out of its misery with my old shotgun. Left it there as an example to the others."

"The others?"

"Abbott and Costello." He smiled. "Here comes one of them now."

A silver disc, looking like a miniature flying saucer, glided across the lawn towards them.

"Automatic lawnmowers," said the Colonel. "I've got two of them. They patrol the lawn. They're programmed to know where the edges of the lawn are so that they don't stray into the flower beds. They cut only a little on each outing and deposit the cuttings back onto the lawn as compost, then they make their way back to their charging stations to recharge on solar power. All very eco-friendly."

The disc buzzed past them. I wonder what Boswell and Hodge would make of that, Agatha thought — scrap metal, probably.

"Amazing," she said, making an attempt to appear interested.

"Now what was it that you wanted to talk to me about, young lady?"

Agatha glanced over her shoulder, half expecting to see Toni standing there. Young lady? He meant her! The Colonel was turning out to be a bit of a charmer.

"Show-jumping," she smiled, "and murder." She explained about Charles and how he had been accused of Mary's murder.

"I heard about that," the Colonel said, scratching his beard. Agatha noticed that the tips of two fingers on his right hand were missing. "Nasty business. I've met Sir Charles a few times over the years. Seems like a decent sort."

"He is indeed," Agatha agreed, "absolutely decent. No doubt about it. A decent sort."

The front door stood open, inviting them into a hall where the walls were hung with framed photographs of soldiers posing with horses in an assortment of exotic locations as well as with camels in the desert, elephants in the jungle and all sorts of military hardware.

"My study will be best." The Colonel held

165

open the door to a wood-panelled room dominated by a desk not unlike the one in Agatha's office. A large, thick ledger with a well-worn green leather cover lay in the middle of the desk. Agatha sat in a deep-buttoned dark-red leather armchair and the Colonel settled into a similar chair on the other side of the desk, fishing a smartphone out of his pocket and placing it beside the ledger.

"So how can I be of help, my dear?" he asked.

"In order to find the killer, I need to know more about Mary, about her friends and, more particularly, her enemies. I'm focusing on those involved in competitive show-jumping. Tamara Montgomery told me you knew absolutely everyone."

"That is true," the Colonel said, touching one of his truncated fingers on the smart-phone screen. The ledger magically opened, revealing a laptop computer inside. He clearly enjoyed Agatha's look of amazement. "Cool, eh? That's what you young people say, isn't it?"

"Very impressive," Agatha conceded.

"Obviously you know that I'm heavily involved in organising events," he turned the ledger so that the laptop screen faced towards him, "but the lists of names and contacts I have here are strictly on a need-to-know basis. It would be thoroughly bad form for me to share."

"We already have lists of Mary's acquaintances," Agatha explained, avoiding using the word "friends," as she seriously doubted Mary had had any of those. "I really need to know more about what went on at these events so that I can work out who might have wanted to murder . . . Lady Mary." She used Mary's title deliberately, hoping that a show of respect for rank would go down well with the Colonel.

"I don't really concern myself with tittle-tattle and barrack-room gossip," he said, "but I will help as much as I can. I'll just see if my wife can rustle something up for us." He prodded his phone with a blunt finger. There was a click as an invisible intercom system switched on. "Jen, how about some tea and biscuits?"

"Thanks," came a voice from loudspeakers somewhere in the room. "I'd love some."

Click.

"Not really the plan. Still, best plans never survive contact with the enemy, eh?" The Colonel chuckled. "Adapt and survive. How about this instead?" He jabbed another icon on his phone screen, and a section of wooden panelling behind him opened up, revealing a drinks cabinet. "A little sherry, maybe?"

"That would be very nice," Agatha smiled. "Where do all these high-tech gizmos come from?"

"Most of them I build myself," the Colonel explained, pouring them both a drink from a crystal decanter. "Spent my working years in the Royal Electrical and Mechanical Engineers. I've always loved horses, of course, but I think I've always loved machines and gadgets just a little bit more. The future is high-tech, young lady."

He handed a glass to Agatha and saw her looking at his fingers.

"Wounded in action," he said, holding up his hand.

"Were you shot?"

"No, rotor blades got me. I stepped out of a helicopter and saluted my generals."

"With two fingers? That wasn't a very nice salute."

"They weren't very nice generals."

"Just as well they weren't your privates . . ."

The Colonel chuckled. "I like you," he said. "If I were forty years younger . . ."

"I'd be a schoolgirl and you'd be arrested."

He guffawed with laughter and gently

clinked glasses with Agatha before lowering himself into his seat again.

"All I can really tell you," he said, "is that Mary Darlinda Brown-Field was a young woman with a lot of problems. She could be very charming, but she also had a knack of upsetting people. I'm sure you know that already."

"First-hand experience," Agatha agreed, "but I have no real experience of the sort of competition environment at show-jumping events, or the people involved. I've only ever been to one small charity event."

"The big events are quite something." He nodded. "The international scene is for the super-rich. Jen and I are, you might say, comfortably well off, with my army pension and some family money, but those who compete at the top events live a lifestyle that most can only dream of."

"Is Claudette one of those?"

"Claudette Duvivier? Do you know Claudette?"

"No, but I would very much like to meet her."

"Let me see what I can do," he said, picking up his phone. He chose a number from a speed-dial list and Agatha listened patiently to a one-sided conversation. "Claudette, my dear! Yes, yes, I'm looking forward to it. Yes, Jen will be coming, too. Claudette, I have someone here who would love to meet you. Her name is Agatha Raisin. Really? *La dame* what? All right . . ." He covered the phone with one hand and spoke softly to Agatha. "She wants to know if you are *la dame d'âne* . . . the Donkey Lady."

"*La dame* . . . Yes," Agatha admitted, taking a gulp of sherry. "That's me. I didn't realise I was famous in France."

The Colonel gave a Gallic shrug and returned to the conversation. "Yes, that's her." There was a pause. "If that's what you want, my dear. I'll check." He covered the phone again and addressed Agatha. "Are you free to go on a little trip on Friday and Saturday? Claudette would love to meet you. I'd say yes if I were you."

"Then yes," said Agatha.

"She can." The Colonel resumed his phone conversation. "Very well. Friday morning. ETA with you at the mill at ten hundred hours. Bella? Yes, I can bring Bella if your chap can look after her at the airport. That's a splendid idea. Perfect weather for her. *Au revoir,* my dear."

He put down his phone and beamed at Agatha.

"We're going on a trip?" Agatha asked. "Where are we going?"

"To meet Claudette," he said.

"I know you like springing little surprises," said Agatha, gesturing towards the laptop and the drinks cabinet, "but if this is on a need-to-know basis, then I am surely one of the ones who need to know."

"You'll need your passport and a couple of posh frocks for dinner," he advised. "You're coming with us to Bordeaux."

CHAPTER SIX

"Surprises are all very well, guys," Agatha said, holding a black sequinned evening gown against herself while standing in front of the full-length mirror in her bedroom, "but a surprise trip at short notice gives a girl no chance to decide what to pack, does it?"

She turned to face them and Boswell and Hodge stared at her from the bed, their eyes wide, tails flicking. "You don't care, do you? You just want to be fed." Agatha draped the dress over the stool by her dressing table and made her way downstairs to the kitchen, the cats trotting at her heels. She fed her feline companions before turning her attention to her own evening meal, pouring herself a glass of red to help her consider the options. She had an individual steak-and-kidney pie in the fridge and, somewhere in the freezer, a box of microwaveable oven chips. She'd nuke the pie as well. The pastry would go floppy, but she didn't care. There was more to think about than dainty cooking.

Sitting at the kitchen table, she sipped wine and opened the pad normally used to make shopping lists. Who would want Mary dead? Keep an open mind, she told herself. Don't rule anything out. Let's start with those closest to home.

Darell and Linda. Perhaps the most unlikely suspects. They really have nothing to gain from Mary's death. Maybe a business associate might have an axe to grind or profit to make with Mary out of the way? Patrick might have come up with something on that front.

Charles. Probably still the main focus of the police investigation, but certainly not guilty of murdering Mary. Chief Inspector Wilkes, however, might be working on the assumption that Charles paid someone to do the deed — a professional hit man. Can you still say "hit man" nowadays, or is that too gender-specific? Should it be "hit person?" Ridiculous. In any case, a pro would surely have kept it clean and would never have risked being discovered setting up the bizarre suicide-in-riding-gear scenario. Nevertheless, Charles is still a police suspect.

Gustav. He would do anything for Charles. Yet Charles would never sanction Mary's murder. He would always have wanted to find another way to deal with the Brown-Field problem. Gustav would know that. Despite the fact that the Brown-Fields might force him out of Barfield House, Gustav wouldn't risk doing something as awful as committing murder if he thought it would turn Charles against him. It would be interesting, however, to find out a bit more about his mysterious background. He's still a police suspect at the very least. We need to check if he has an alibi.

Mrs. Tassy. There's no way she had anything to do with Mary's murder, however much she loathed the Brown-Fields. The whole idea is simply beneath her dignity, and she's not strong enough to have done it anyway. Impossible. Only Wilkes would ever be stupid enough to consider her as a suspect or that she might be acting in league with Gustav.

Me. Well, I know I didn't do it. Wilkes might think differently, but I don't need to waste any time investigating myself.

The microwave pinged. She took the chips out and put the pie in. She shook the chips out of their box onto a plate and tried one. Too hot. She sucked in some air to cool her mouth and took a sip of wine, returning to her list. What about the horse-riding lot? she asked herself. Toni, Patrick or Simon may have been able to come up with someone from the party list, but in the meantime, we have:

Tamara Montgomery. She was blackmailed by Mary and had her business trashed by Mary and her father. Plenty of motive. She didn't seem like a murderer, but that means nothing. Her alibi has to be verified. "Things," Agatha said out loud, mimicking John Cornish's accent, "ain't always what they seem." The Colonel's computer masquerading as a ledger certainly wasn't, which brings me on to . . .

Claudette Duvivier. We know nothing about her. That's something I need to sort out before I meet her on Friday. She knows who I am. I need to know all I can about her, too.

Deborah Lexington. Again, I know nothing about her, but we should know more by tomorrow. I will have to pay her a visit.

Mrs. Chadwick. Might she have been involved? She is linked to Mary through Darell and the horse brooch, but does she have a motive for murder? Could Mary have been blackmailing her too?

The truth is, Agatha decided, everywhere

we turn, another suspect crops up.

The microwave pinged again and she scooped the collapsed pie onto the plate with her chips. It was not an appetising sight, but she was too hungry to care. She reached into a cupboard for some ketchup to brighten up the meal, then heard the front door opening.

"Coo-ee!" came the voice of Roy Silver. He struggled up the hall and stood in the kitchen doorway laden with carrier bags. "Can we pop down to the Red Lion, darling? My treat. I'm famished and I couldn't possibly even consider showing you all these fabulous things without something to eat and a decent drink."

"I'll get my coat," said Agatha, scraping the pie and chips into the bin.

The Raisin Investigations staff were in the office the following morning bright and early. They all assembled round Agatha's desk and she explained that Roy would not be joining them as he was on special assignment at the stables. She then handed Toni the page from her notebook.

"The list of suspects is growing," she informed everyone. "Read this out, please, Toni, so we can recap."

"Eggs, tissues, milk, cat food . . ."

"The bottom bit!" groaned Agatha, rolling her eyes.

Toni giggled and went through the list of names. Patrick Mulligan chipped in.

"I've got quite a lot of background on Mary from various police contacts," he said. "She has been cautioned a couple of times following disturbances at show-jumping events. A retired mate of mine has been working in security at some of the events and he says she has a bad reputation for getting into fights with other competitors, but charges have always been dropped.

"One of those fights was with Deborah Lexington. She lives with her brother in a house near a village called Duns Tew. Their parents died in a hotel fire in Turkey several years ago.

"Deborah says she caught Mary trying to feed something to her horse. At these events, you don't go anywhere near anyone else's horses without express permission or in the company of the owner. Deborah claimed that Mary was trying to nobble her horse — to drug or poison it. She grabbed hold of her and dragged her away. There was a lot of screaming and shouting and a bit of a cat fight before Mary shoved Deborah."

"I've been on the receiving end of one of

those shoves," said Agatha. "She packed a lot of power into them."

"Deborah staggered back, tripped and hit her head on a Land Rover tow bar. She was badly hurt — ended up in a coma. When she finally woke, she was partly paralysed. At one point, doctors expected that she would recover fully, but she never has."

"Why didn't Mary go to jail for that?" asked Simon.

"There were no actual witnesses," Patrick explained. "Some people heard a commotion, but it was all over very quickly. Deborah's brother was the one who found her. When she came round, it was Deborah's word against Mary's. Mary said Deborah must have fallen and that she was fine when she left her. No trace of any poison or drugs was ever found in the horse."

"Wow," gasped Toni. "If anybody had a motive to murder Mary, it was Deborah Lexington."

"But she's not physically capable of doing it," said Agatha. "Still, we should pay her a visit. Have you been keeping an eye on Mrs. Chadwick, Simon, and did you find out any more about the horse brooch?"

"The house that Mrs. Chadwick and Darell use in Oxford has been empty all week," said Simon. "Neither of them has been near the place. According to Mr. Chadwick, his wife has gone abroad and isn't expected back until the beginning of next week.

"As far as the brooch is concerned, I spoke to a jewellery designer here in Mircester. He put me on to a London jeweller, who identified the brooch as one of her creations. She said that she made one for a particular client — wouldn't say who — as a special birthday present for her daughter. A few weeks later the girl's father commissioned an exact copy. Said his wife liked his daughter's brooch so much that she wanted one as well. Those are the only two in existence."

"I'm betting Mrs. Chadwick spotted Mary's brooch," said Agatha, "and demanded that Darell get her one as well."

"She must mean a lot to him," said Simon. "Best estimate I could get for the cost of the brooch is five to ten thousand pounds."

"That's peanuts to Darell," said Patrick. "The Brown-Field business empire is worth countless millions. They started out manufacturing ladies' . . . um . . . sanitary products, but they have diversified with all sorts of investments in property and the leisure industry.

"Darell is a keen golfer. He plays in Spain

and is a member of at least two golf clubs in the UK. Just like his daughter, he likes to win and doesn't always play fair. He was kicked out of one club for cheating but was back again a couple of weeks later. When they told him he wasn't welcome, he simply said, 'I think you'll find I am.' One of his companies had bought the club. Basically, he owned the place.

"Rumour has it that his golfing cronies include some senior police officers. That may be part of the reason why no charges against Mary ever stuck. He is also known for having ways of getting to people, either through straightforward bribes or by using strong-arm tactics — scaring people off with hired help."

"Good work, guys," said Agatha. She knew she could be a difficult boss, but she also believed in giving credit where it was due. "I need you two to stay on top of our other cases, but try to track down some of those riders who were on the receiving end of Mary's foul temper at competitions. They may not have pressed charges, but we need to know who they were and whether they could have been involved in her murder."

"I think the police are already doing that," said Patrick.

"I suppose they had to be one step ahead

of us somewhere," said Agatha. "Follow up nonetheless. We don't want to miss anything. As a priority, I need some background on a Frenchwoman named Claudette Duvivier. She appears to be a regular on the show-jumping circuit. I'm meeting her tomorrow and want to know a bit about her. Toni, you and I will pay a visit to Deborah Lexington today. All right, let's get to it."

Later that morning, Agatha and Toni set off for Duns Tew, with Toni driving. They headed for Chipping Norton, then took the road towards Banbury before turning right onto a series of minor roads that grew ever narrower the farther they ventured. The low hedgerows and regular copses of trees marked the boundaries of fields that spread as far as the eye could see. Scatterings of sheep, dazzling white in the sunshine, were the only signs of life save for the sparse clusters of farm buildings. The old mellow stone buildings stood quietly, in perfect harmony with the scenery, but on crossing a bridge over a stream, Toni spotted two low, angular, overgrown concrete structures, one either side of the road.

"Those are funny little sheds," she said.

"Not sheds," said Agatha. "Charles has a few of those on his estate. They're pillboxes

— gun emplacements left over from the Second World War. You know what a history buff he is. He says there were almost thirty thousand of them all over the country to help fight the Nazis had they invaded. Most of them have been bulldozed by now, but he won't let anyone touch his."

"I think we must be nearly there," said Toni, and the road swept into a hamlet that Agatha deemed a pleasant mix of old and more modern stone houses. They passed the White Horse Inn before finding a side road that led them to what was clearly a fairly new, late-twentieth-century house with a large front garden. The five-bar wooden gates in front of the driveway stood closed, with a red Ford hatchback parked on the drive. They left their car by the narrow pavement and walked through a smaller garden gate set in the white picket fence. By the time they reached the front door, a young man was standing waiting for them.

"Can I help you?" he asked, with a welcoming smile.

"We're looking for Deborah Lexington," Agatha explained. "We'd like to talk to her."

"I'm not sure you can right now," he said. "Come in and I'll see if she's up to having visitors."

He waved them into the hall. Agatha

judged him to be in his late twenties, and by the way his white T-shirt clung to his frame, he was in very good shape. Tall, lean and well muscled. She spotted Toni checking him out as well.

"I'm Jacob," he said, giving each of them a firm handshake. "Jake — Debbie's brother. Let me check if she's awake."

He disappeared into a room on the left, closing the door behind him. Agatha looked around. The decor was painfully bland and modern. The walls and ceiling were painted white and the floor was covered with a beige carpet. A white wooden staircase wound its way from the far end of the hall to the upper floor. Toni quickly walked forward and squinted up the stairs, then through to the rooms at the rear of the house. She ran a hand across some mail sitting on a wooden table by the foot of the stairs. Opposite the room into which Jake had gone was what would have been a family lounge, but through the open door Agatha could see that it was laid out with gym equipment, weights and a couple of large computer screens. Window blinds reduced the late-morning sunshine to bars of light on the floor.

"My den." Jake had returned. "I'm a website designer and I like to work out.

Makes sense to have it all in the same room. Debbie is ready for you now."

Agatha and Toni were shown into a room that would once have been a dining room but was now more of a hospital suite. A large steel bed dominated the white room, and a pale, thin woman lay between crisp white sheets, propped up with pillows. On her left, two monitors blinked discreetly, the wires that snaked from them towards the bed no doubt attached to the patient somewhere beneath her pink silk pyjama top. To her right, a vase of fresh flowers stood on a side table, along with a TV remote control, a paperback novel, a glass of water and a bottle of perfume.

"Help me up a little more, Jake," she said, and the young man stepped forward. She draped her left arm around his shoulders, and he eased her forward, pressing a button at the side of the bed to raise it behind her back.

"I'm Deborah Lexington." She held out her left hand to Agatha. "The other one's not much use any more."

Agatha shook her hand. The skin felt warm and she noticed small beads of sweat on Deborah's brow.

"I'm Agatha Raisin, and this —"

"Yes, I know who you both are," said Deborah, "and I've heard what you're up to. I may be stuck in this bed but my friends keep me up to date with what's going on in the real world."

"Then you know why we want to talk to you," said Agatha. Jacob offered her and Toni two seats by the bed. Toni produced a notepad and pen.

"You want to talk about darling Mary Darlinda," Deborah sneered. "The most hateful human being ever to walk the face of the earth — may she rot in hell."

Toni looked up from her pad.

"Do I shock you?" Deborah asked, tilting her head meekly in mock innocence.

"Not at all," said Agatha. "I think I understand why —"

"Understand?" roared Deborah. "How can you possibly understand? How can you even begin to understand what it's like to wake up one morning and find that you've lost the use of your legs and your right arm? You can't possibly understand how it feels to be trapped in this bloody bed with only that," she pointed to the television screen hanging on the wall opposite, "and a crummy phone to keep you in touch with life outside — with what all your friends are getting up to!"

She fanned herself with her left hand and

waved Jacob towards the perfume bottle.

"I'm sorry," said Agatha. "You're right. I can't begin to imagine what you've been through."

"Calms me down," said Deborah, squirting perfume into the air around her. "Used to stop me smelling of horses; now it stops me smelling of me. And you're wrong."

"I'm wrong? How?"

"You CAN begin to imagine. At least you can imagine how it began." Deborah laughed. "I heard she sent you flying just like she did me. Gave you a bit of a champagne shower."

"You are very well informed."

"Hell, no — everybody's been talking about that night. Friends of mine came to see me before the infamous masked ball. One of them showed me her invitation. Said she wouldn't go, of course, after what Mary did to me . . . but she went anyway. She saw the whole thing between you and Mary. The Battle of Barfield House, they're calling it."

"It wasn't much of a battle really," said Agatha, "but it did help to get me arrested for murder."

"Obviously you didn't do it," Deborah smirked, "even though I bet you would have liked to after she snatched your lovely Sir

Charles away from you."

"I had no reason at all to like Mary, but —"

"But you didn't kill her because you were halfway down the drive having a heart-to-heart with Sir Charles. You were seen. You had about as much chance of strangling the bitch that night as I did."

"If it wasn't you and it wasn't Agatha, then who was it?" Toni interjected. She had put down her pad and had started tinkering with her phone. Agatha scowled at her.

"How should I know?" said Deborah. "You're the detectives. Get out there and detect! Let me know if you find who did it and I'll give him a medal. Now go. I'm feeling tired."

Jacob ushered them out to the hall. Toni took a step into his den.

"Is this where you spend all your time?" she asked. "Do you ever go out . . . socialising?"

"I work mainly from home," he said. "I go out to meetings from time to time, and to do a little shopping, but having everything here means that I'm on hand when Debbie needs me."

"Can she be left on her own?" said Toni.

"A nurse comes in. I'm able to go out then."

"With your muscles," she smiled, running a finger over a dumb-bell, "I'd have thought you could manage far heavier weights than this."

"Bit of a pectoral strain," Jacob explained, gently rubbing his chest. "I'm taking it easy."

"You need to be careful," she said, looking round the room. "This is a lovely house."

"Not as big as the house we were brought up in, but it suits us. We moved here when our parents died. Then there was Debbie's accident . . ."

"That must have been awful for you."

"Toni," hissed Agatha, growing increasingly impatient with Toni's flirting. "It's time we were going."

Toni wound down the car windows as Agatha fastened her seat belt. The sun had made the inside of the vehicle unbearably hot.

"Phew!" she said, starting the engine. "It's like a furnace in here. They say there's a change in the weather coming next week. It won't be so hot."

"Thank you for the weather forecast," said Agatha, "but it's not only hot in here. It was getting pretty steamy in there too. What on earth were you playing at? 'Do you ever go out?' and 'You could manage far heavier weights.' We're supposed to be working, finding things out, not fishing for dates."

"I was finding things out." Toni giggled. "Come on, it's nearly lunchtime — let me buy you a long, cool drink!"

It took only moments for them to retrace their route back to Duns Tew, where Toni pulled into the car park behind the White Horse. At the rear of the inn, wooden tables bathed in the sunshine, but while a cold drink in the garden was an attractive option, when they went inside, the cool flagstones on the floor were irresistible. Agatha kicked off her shoes and let her feet enjoy the chill of the stones.

"Food here looks great," said Toni, picking up a menu.

"Just a gin and tonic for me," said Agatha, sucking in her stomach. "I'm still a little full from yet another meal at the Red Lion last night. You'd best have a lemonade — designated driver."

She took a look around while Toni ordered their drinks. The bar area was quiet, but the White Horse had the look of a place that never stayed quiet for long. The heavy wooden beams sported traditional horse brasses but the exposed stone walls were hung with quirky modern artwork, creating an atmosphere in the seventeenth-century inn that made Agatha want to settle in for the duration. In the past, on one of those days she sometimes spent drifting through the Cotswold countryside with Charles, they probably would have stayed all afternoon. They probably would have booked a room for the night. Those days, however, were definitely in the past. She took a seat at a small table and planted her feet on the cool floor. Toni delivered the drinks.

"So if you weren't trying to snare young Jake," said Agatha, "what were you up to in there?"

"The house has the look of a place that is pretty much empty," said Toni. "It felt odd. The kitchen and what looked like a garden room at the back of the house were unfurnished."

"Maybe not so odd," said Agatha. "Deborah must practically live in that room. Jake has the rest of the house. Too many bedrooms, too much space for a young guy. Why should he care about furnishing it all?"

"It looked like it had been furnished, though. There were furniture marks on the carpet in his den, and if he and Deborah came from a bigger house after the death of their parents, you would expect them to bring lots of furniture with them. I think the house has been cleared."

"What do you mean?"

"Take a look at this." Toni handed Agatha her smartphone. "The mail on the table at the bottom of the stairs looked like it came from lawyers and estate agents. Then I found this online."

On Toni's phone screen was a photograph of the house they had just left. The picture was on an estate agent's website. Agatha scrolled through other pictures of the house. Deborah's room had been photographed without her bed or monitors. Jacob's den had neither gym equipment nor computer screens. The other rooms were equally bare. The house looked unoccupied.

"Looks like it's ready for a buyer to move straight in," said Agatha.

"Ideal for a quick sale," agreed Toni, "and it has been sold. Look at the price."

Agatha was surprised by the seven-figure sale price. She was well aware of the high property values in this part of the country, but that was a huge sum for a house like the Lexingtons.

"That will put a lot of cash in their pockets," she said. "Certainly enough to hire someone to take revenge on Mary."

"It's still a weird and risky kind of contract

killing," Toni said, "and we don't know what their financial situation is. We don't know how much Deborah's medical care may be costing them."

"Then we must find out." Agatha sipped her drink. "Or rather you must. I need to see Charles this afternoon and update him. Come on, let's find a shady spot to finish these drinks in the garden."

Toni dropped Agatha at home before heading into the office. Agatha phoned Barfield House to check that Charles was home. Gustav answered.

"What do you want?" he grunted.

"Really, Gustav," Agatha scolded him. "You could try to be a bit nicer to me. We are still on the same side, after all."

"The way things are," said Gustav, "I can trust no one. Sides mean nothing."

"Is Charles at home this afternoon? I want to come and see him."

"I believe so. I will warn him."

"Thank you, Gustav. Every phone call with you fills me with joy . . . as soon as I hang up."

There was a click. He'd beaten her to it.

Agatha took a quick shower, reapplied her make-up and picked out a sky-blue crêpe dress with a delicate yellow flower pattern, a low V neck and cinched sleeves. A thin belt at the waist made it ideal for her figure. It was summery, but she was seeing Charles, not just any ordinary client, and if Toni the weather girl was right, then the fine weather was due to end and summer could fast be fading into the distant future again. This dress deserved to be worn in the sunshine, and now was the time to do it.

She was halfway down the garden path, heading for her car, when she heard James calling to her. He was standing in the doorway of his cottage, a book in one hand and a teacup in the other, as always.

"Aggie, are you off out, darling?" he said. "That's a splendid dress."

"Thank you, James. In a bit of a hurry. Off to see Charles."

"Oh, right . . . Er, wondered if you fancied dinner tonight. I'll cook."

"Something light maybe," said Agatha, feeling the belt quite tight around her middle. "I have to be up early tomorrow."

"A salade Niçoise, then!" James grinned. "I have just the wine to go with it."

"Oh, but I have Roy staying."

"Well, I suppose . . . Roy is welcome too, naturally."

"Lovely. Talk later."

James sauntered back into his living room

and sat down with his book. He found himself staring at the pages without reading. Romantic notions had never come easily to him. He had always been solidly pragmatic rather than wildly sentimental, and that little episode on the doorstep had ably demonstrated the wisdom of his ways. Somehow his attempt to conjure up a romantic dinner for two had resulted in a friendly dinner for three. Still, Roy wasn't such a bad chap, and Aggie had looked very attractive in that blue dress. She was, of course, wearing it to meet another man, Charles, who, now that his wife was out of the way, was presumably back on the market again.

He snapped his book shut. If there was a challenge to be faced, he wasn't about to shy away from it. Sir Charles Fraith could not dodge in and out of Agatha's life as he pleased. Whatever mess she was trying to extricate reckless, unreliable Charles from, he had to make it clear that she would always have steadfast, dependable James to fall back on. So . . . dinner for three, then.

On arriving at Barfield House, Agatha decided to avoid the frustration of another encounter with Gustav. Rather than ring the doorbell, she walked round to the terrace at the side of the house. At this time of day, she knew precisely where Charles would be.

The French doors to the library stood open to encourage any breeze that might choose to drift in from the lawn. Agatha paused in the doorway.

"Charles, there's some strange woman on the terrace." The reedy descant of Mrs. Tassy shredded the atmosphere like a dagger drawn down a window pane. Agatha sighed and shook her head. Mrs. Tassy knew exactly who she was. Referring to her as "some strange woman" was the old lady's way of making it known that she disapproved of Agatha arriving in an unorthodox manner, unannounced. Mrs. Tassy sat tall in a wing-backed chair, her crown of silver hair framing her grey face. Her high-necked, long-sleeved black dress reached almost to her ankles, conceding nothing to the spring heatwave. She tutted at Agatha and returned to the book she was reading.

Charles looked up from the paperwork on his desk. Silhouetted in the doorway, with the sun behind her, the pleasing outline of Agatha's body was visible through the fabric of her dress. He smiled.

"I take it the Brown-Fields are absent," said Agatha, nodding towards Mrs. Tassy, "if the undead have resurfaced?"

"At their London flat," said Charles. "Come in and grab a seat, Aggie. I'll get us a drink." He rang a small handbell on his desk and called towards the open library door. "GUSTAV!"

Gustav duly appeared and glowered at Agatha.

"Oh . . . *you* are here," he grumbled.

"Oh . . ." Agatha mimicked him, examining her arms as if to check, then giving him a shrug, "so I am."

Charles asked Gustav to bring them gin and tonics. "And a sherry for the wraith," added the old lady.

"Aunt, Agatha and I need to talk about her investigation," said Charles.

"Go ahead," said Mrs. Tassy. "I have been persecuted and ostracised in this house for months. I refuse to be banished from this room. I am reading a book, and this is the library, where one reads books."

Agatha started to bring Charles up to date. She decided to keep the relationship between Darell and Mrs. Chadwick under wraps for the moment, but explained about Tamara and then mentioned Deborah Lexington. Gustav appeared with their drinks.

"Will that be all?" he asked. "Or are other guests likely to materialise?"

"That will be all, Gustav," said Charles,

then turned back to Agatha. "Lexington . . . I'm sure my father had friends by that name."

"Would that be the Idbury Lexingtons?" came the voice of Mrs. Tassy. "They used to visit when you were away at school, Charles, or up at Cambridge. The girl, Deborah, was a teenager by then, the boy slightly younger — Jason, I believe . . ."

"Jacob," said Agatha.

"Yes, yes, that's what I said — Jacob. It was rather nice seeing children playing on the lawn. They were full of vigour, full of life. They used to lead poor Gustav a merry dance. Played all sorts of tricks on him. They stopped coming after the parents died in a dreadful fire at a hotel in Greece . . ."

"Turkey," said Agatha.

"Yes, yes, of course," said the old lady tetchily. "She does like to contradict, does she not, Charles?"

"It's Agatha's job to get things like that right," Charles laughed.

Agatha explained about Deborah's altercation with Mary.

"You knew nothing about that?" she asked.

"Didn't know Mary then," Charles explained, "and you know that I've never taken any interest in the horsey crowd."

"It's strange that the Lexingtons used to visit all those years ago," said Agatha.

"Lots of people used to visit," said Charles. "It's just a coincidence."

"In a murder investigation, we can't afford to write things off as coincidence. Coincidences are highly suspicious."

"You consider Deborah Lexington a suspect?"

"A fairly unlikely suspect, given her circumstances," Agatha admitted. "We're still looking at her and Tamara and . . . Well, there won't be any shortage of suspects. I'm meeting another person of interest tomorrow. A Frenchwoman, Claudette Duvivier."

"How is her English?" asked Charles, sounding keen to get involved. "I could translate, if you like."

"It's best if you're not involved," Agatha said, "and we are apparently off to Bordeaux."

"Is that going to be at my expense?"

"No, Charles, I have been invited. It appears to be a freebie."

"Careful. There's no such thing as a free lunch."

"You of all people should know that's not true!" Agatha laughed. "I've lost count of the free lunches and dinners that you and your elusive wallet have wangled. Whoops!"

she added, glancing at her watch. "Is that the time? I should be going."

"Let me walk you to your car," offered Charles.

They strolled together in the sunshine, pausing for a moment to take in the view over the lawn to the mature parkland beyond. At the car, Charles slipped his arm around Agatha's shoulder.

"Thank you for everything you're doing," he said. "I would be lost without you." He leaned in to kiss her, but she turned her face away and the kiss landed on her ear.

"Steady, tiger," she said gently. "Let's keep this a professional relationship. Otherwise one or both of us could yet end up in jail."

She stepped into the car and headed for home.

CHAPTER SEVEN

Agatha arrived home to a rapturous reception from Boswell and Hodge. They miaowed and purred and wound themselves around her legs.

"Take it easy, guys," she said, stooping to stroke each in turn. "I know this is cupboard love — you just want to be fed. Come on, then." The cats pranced in front of her, tails high, heading for the kitchen. No sooner had she filled their food bowls than she heard the front door creaking open. There was a low groan of pain and a stagger of footsteps. Agatha rushed into the hall. Roy Silver stood there, face flushed, legs wide apart, supporting himself with one hand on the banisters and the other on the living room door frame. He was wearing pale-blue jodhpurs, a dark-blue polo shirt with a horse motif, and a look of excruciating discomfort.

"It's agony, Aggie!" he wailed. "I shall

never be able to close my legs again. No jokes, please."

"What on earth has happened to you?" Agatha held a hand to her face to cover a smile.

"Riding . . . had my first riding lesson with Tamara. I thought you just sat there and held onto the reins. Turns out you have to balance, sit up straight, move with the horse . . . My legs haven't ached like this since that time you made me run a marathon."

"It was a five-kilometre charity fun run, Roy, and you walked it."

"While you were schmoozing with the sponsor."

"It was a team effort."

"I need a long soak in a hot bath," he said, starting to climb the stairs.

"I'll get you a glass of wine," said Agatha. "I take it your riding days are over?"

"Not at all!" he called, reaching the top of the stairs. "I'll be back in the saddle tomorrow. Loved every second of it. It's just a shame we have to suffer so much for life's pleasures . . ."

"James has invited us round for supper," Agatha called after him.

"Not for me," came the reply. "I really don't feel up to it."

Agatha called James to let him know Roy would not be joining them. She was sure she could detect a note of relief in his voice. She opened a bottle of Chablis that had been chilling in the fridge and took a glass upstairs for Roy. The bathroom door stood slightly ajar.

"Roy, I've got a glass of wine for you."

"Oh, you are an angel! Bring it in. Don't worry, I'm totally bubbled."

She peered round the door to see Roy luxuriating in her bath, steam rising through a mountain of white froth. She handed him the wine glass and he took a sip before letting his drinking arm loll over the side of the tub.

"Ah, bliss," he said. "That was a busy day, you know. We've been talking to potential sponsors and made a start on a mail-out to possible clients."

"Anything new I should know about Tamara?"

"She had a friend stay over last night. There was a car at the stables this morning and she was washing up plates and glasses when I arrived. I'm pretty sure it was a male friend, but she wasn't telling. She was a bit coy about it. You know, when she took off that old baggy sweater to lead Saturn while I bounced around on his back, she was wearing a T-shirt and she actually has a remarkably trim figure. Clearly very fit and strong."

"Well, keeping fit isn't a crime. Neither is having a man friend. That certainly doesn't make her a murderer."

"It doesn't make her innocent, either."

"You're right. She's still a suspect. Keep your ear to the ground there, Roy. Try to have a word with the people who help Tamara at the stables, too. They might put us on to another lead. Right — I'm off next door."

James Lacey's cottage bore a strong resemblance to Agatha's, a family resemblance that, as with most family likenesses, went little more than skin deep. The appearance and layout of the two houses might have been similar, but they were entirely different in character.

When Agatha had first moved in to her cottage, she had an interior designer decorate and furnish the whole place to make it look like the sort of idyllic country home that appeared in glossy newspaper supplements. It didn't matter that the supplements were only ever read by bored commuters stuck on delayed trains that had left one of London's stations and were going nowhere.

Being in one of those articles was what counted. That was the way to show everyone she had left behind in London what a wonderful new life she was enjoying. She had wanted them all to be jealous — even the bored commuters she had never met. Her cottage never made it into a glossy magazine, and it now had a far more comfortable, lived-in feel. She had slowly transformed it from an idyllic country home into *her* home, and she no longer cared about impressing anyone in London. Well, not with her fixtures and fittings at least. She still wanted everyone to know that she was living a life they should envy — even the anonymous commuters — but her cottage was her own private space.

James's cottage was a different kind of private space. Things had a tendency to drift around in Agatha's cottage. An ornament might be in the dining room one week, moved on a whim to the living room the next, and in a charity shop the week after. James was a former military man, and in his cottage, everything remained in its proper place, neatly regimented, unless orders were received to mobilise. Books stood smartly to attention on shelves as straight as a sergeant major's swagger stick. Agatha could never understand how he got everything to stay that way. In her place, the floors, walls and ceilings seemed to compete for the title of "Wonkiest Surface." She was pleasantly surprised, therefore, when James showed her into his small dining room.

On a day-to-day basis, the dining room served as James's study. These days he was a moderately successful travel writer, and this was where his latest insights on far-flung places were whipped into shape. Tonight, however, the disciplined order of the study had been swept away. The desk had been transformed into a table for two, set with a crisp white cloth and two tall candles.

"James, you've gone to so much trouble," was all Agatha could think to say.

"No, no trouble . . . well, a bit, obviously . . . but not *so* much . . ."

"It looks lovely," she said, and reached up to kiss him on the cheek. He grinned. His face was tanned from exotic foreign travel and his blue eyes shone from beneath dark brows. A sweep of grey at the sides of his thick black hair was the only real sign of advancing years, and he stood tall and unbowed. He looked as handsome as the day he had moved into Lilac Lane and set all the village women's hearts aflutter. Yet it was Agatha Raisin who had been the one to snare him. "It makes me feel very special."

"You are special," he said, pulling out her chair for her. "So I thought this should be special. Wouldn't really have worked for three . . ."

He poured the wine and took his seat.

"Aggie, I've been meaning to talk to you about . . ." A timer pinged somewhere in the kitchen. "Garlic bread."

"You want to talk to me about garlic bread?"

"No, no, not that. Garlic bread's ready in the oven. I'd best take it out."

He left the room and a cold sensation spread across Agatha's shoulders. Then her heart dropped into her stomach. The table, she thought to herself, the candles . . . this is all so *romantic*. A romantic atmosphere was definitely not the environment normally inhabited by James Lacey. Oh my God! He's going to propose! Or re-propose, or whatever it is people do when they get remarried!

James returned with a basket of bread and an ornate dish adorned with a carefully prepared salad.

"James, this is all very romantic," said Agatha, "but I hope you're not going to . . ."

"Not going to what?"

"You know, after what we've been discussing . . . with the murder inquiry, this wouldn't be a very good time to . . ."

"Ah, yes . . . ahem! I see," James blustered. "No, nothing like that. I just wanted to talk to you about . . . the investigation. Then I thought, no, let's just relax and . . . um . . . take your mind off it for an evening. How is it all going, by the way?"

Far from taking Agatha's mind off the murder of Lady Mary Fraith, they then talked of nothing else for the rest of the evening. By the time they had polished off their second bottle of wine, Agatha was starting to feel weary. She stifled a yawn.

"You'll have to excuse me, James," she said. "I need to be up early tomorrow for the French trip."

"Absolutely no problem," said James, jumping to his feet and drawing back Agatha's chair for her like an over-eager waiter. They hesitated by the front door and he placed his hands gently on her shoulders. She threw her arms around him and hugged him tight. Then she laughed.

"I really don't need you to play the fawning flunkey, you know," she smiled. "I love the regular James Lacey just the way he is."

He stooped, she eased herself up on her tiptoes and they kissed.

"Thank you for a lovely evening," she said.

"When this awful business is all over, we must talk again . . . about us."

"It's a date," he smiled.

It wasn't her biggest suitcase, but it wasn't her smallest, either. Lying open, it covered far less than half the bed. The Colonel had said she need only be there for a couple of nights. How many outfits did you really need for two nights? Certainly more than could be fitted into the smallest case. She needed first-choice items and backups, shoes, jewellery, make-up . . . Would she need a swimsuit? The weather was even warmer in Bordeaux than here. She packed one just in case, then packed another for safety, laid a lightweight jacket on top of all the other stuff, threw in an extra pair of knickers and slammed the case shut just as her phone buzzed.

It was a message from Toni. She had kept it brief but had avoided using text speak — or txt spk — which she knew Agatha hated.

Simon and Patrick have found no further suspects so far from Mary's past punch-ups. All either out of the country or have other cast-iron alibis.

Still checking out party guests but no clear suspects to date.

Background on C. Duvivier. Age 33. Mother deceased (cancer). Father deceased (heart attack). Owns a vineyard and finance/investment business with her uncle, Pascal Duvivier. Both extremely wealthy and businesses worth many millions.

Should have info on Lexington med care on your return.

Have fun in France!

Toni

So there were no new suspects who could be placed at Barfield House on the night of the murder. That, thought Agatha, doesn't actually mean much. If we rule out the Brown-Fields, Charles, his aunt, Gustav and me, then even those we *are* considering as suspects can't be placed at Barfield House that night. Maybe Claudette Duvivier will be able to shed some light on the matter.

Heaving the suitcase off the bed, she grabbed a wide-brimmed sunhat and made her way downstairs. She lingered in front of the hall mirror, checking that all was well before she left the house. She wore a pleated sleeveless summer dress with a bold jungle pattern and a bolero shrug top to cover her shoulders and upper arms. High-heeled strappy sandals and a green leather clutch bag completed the look. She wouldn't wear the hat unless it was necessary. You could never tell what was happening with your hair once you took off a hat, so it was best never to put one on in the first place. With that, she hauled her suitcase to the car and set off for Maugersbury.

"Bravo!" called the Colonel as she pulled into his driveway twenty minutes later. "Bang on time. Jen! Agatha's here!"

Jennifer Warbler-Dow was locking the front door. She strode over to greet Agatha with a bright, beaming smile.

"Lovely to meet you at last," she said. "Missed you last time you were here." Agatha judged her to be a few years younger than the Colonel. "Did you bring sunglasses?" she asked, fishing a large pair of dark glasses from a pocket in her lightweight cream trouser suit. Quite stylish, thought Agatha, yet practical for travelling. Agatha produced a pair of aviator shades from her clutch bag. "They'll be fine," Jen said approvingly.

"I'll fetch Bella," the Colonel announced and disappeared round the back of the house.

"Here, take this, my dear," said Jen, offering Agatha a silk headscarf and nodding at her sunhat. "That will be gone in no time."

A mechanical stutter, a bang and the roar of an engine announced the imminent arrival of Bella. The Colonel drove into view at the wheel of a large dark-green vintage car with enormous wire-spoked wheels, neither roof nor windows bar a tiny windscreen, and very little in the way of bodywork. A spare wheel was mounted on the side and the giant headlights looked like monstrous bug eyes. It was the sort of car Agatha imagined Mr. Toad driving in *The Wind in the Willows.*

"A 1931 Bentley," shouted Jen, the roar of the engine subsiding to a minor cacophony. "It's his pride and joy."

"Surely we're not going all the way to Bordeaux in that thing, are we?" asked Agatha.

"No," Jen laughed. "Just a short run to Chipping Norton to pick up Claudette, then on to Oxford airport."

"You two ladies climb in," said the Colonel. "Should be room for that suitcase to sit between you. Ours is strapped to the back."

Agatha opened a small rear door that she judged no bigger than a cat flap and heaved her case into the car, climbing in behind it. As she did so, she spotted her lacy black extra knickers hanging out the side. Maybe nobody else would notice them. Jen entered from the other side, picking the Colonel's green ledger off the simple leather seat.

"Have to take care of this," she smiled, setting it on her lap. "He'll pretty much run the whole event in Bordeaux using this."

Agatha held the sunhat in her lap and tied the headscarf under her chin. She felt disturbingly nervous, convinced that she would arrive at Oxford airport with hair like a blow-dried rat and skin like a sand-blasted chimp. And what would be waiting for them there? A First World War biplane? A Zeppelin?

"All set?" called the Colonel. "Then we're off."

Agatha was vaguely aware of him pulling levers and setting switches that, as a more than competent driver of modern cars, were a complete mystery to her, then the old car rumbled out through the gates. They picked up speed on the open road and she slowly started to enjoy the breeze on her face and the invigoration of the fresh air. Before she knew it, she felt a grin begin. Jen reached across to squeeze her arm.

"Not as bad as you thought it was going to be, is it?" she laughed.

Just outside Chipping Norton, they pulled into a side road signposted for Bliss Mill.

The huge building looked like a stately home, with row upon row of windows and a square tower at each corner. Its most prominent feature, however, was a round tower at the front of the building topped with a neat dome out of which, bizarrely, a colossal factory chimney launched itself into the sky, the only real clue that this was a former tweed mill. Agatha had seen the building from the road many times but had never come this close before. She was aware that the old mill was now a development of luxury apartments.

"Why don't you pop up and meet Claudette?" said Jen, waving to a slight figure at a second-floor window. "We'll wait here."

Agatha eased herself out of the car and set off into the mill. Stepping out of the elevator on the second floor, she was greeted by a slim, smiling dark-eyed woman, casually dressed in T-shirt and jeans. Agatha would have judged Claudette Duvivier to be much younger had she not known from the brief background report that she was thirty-three. Her skin was smooth and lightly tanned and her long, glossy hair swept back and forth well below her shoulders with every movement of her head.

"You are Agatha, yes?" She held out her hand. Agatha went to shake it, then realised she was holding the headscarf that she had removed in the elevator. "Aha!" laughed Claudette. "For your hair, yes? How did you enjoy your first journey in Bella?"

"I think I can see how you might get to like Bella," said Agatha, using unaccustomed diplomacy, "but I'm not quite used to her yet."

"She is so beautiful," Claudette enthused, her soft French accent caressing every syllable. "I am so happy when the Colonel brings beautiful Bella. I am almost ready," she added, leading Agatha into her apartment. The exposed brickwork of the walls in the large living area seemed to glow in the sunlight that flooded through the tall windows. Wooden beams separated a series of brick arches that formed the ceiling. The furnishings were modern, but not aggressively so. It was a stunning apartment.

"It is nice here, no?" said Claudette. "I adore to stay here when I am in England."

"It is very nice," agreed Agatha. *Très chic.*"

"Ah, you speak French?"

"No, not really," Agatha admitted, "but I love visiting France, especially Paris."

"Then you will love staying at our house. I can't wait to show you round. But I think that you want to speak to me about something, yes?"

"About Mary Brown-Field."

"Ah, yes, that one." Claudette's smile faded. "It is very sad what happened."

Agatha explained about Charles and the murder investigation.

"I understand that you were not friends with Mary."

Claudette folded a T-shirt into a small suitcase and picked up a riding helmet. A hat box stood open, ready to accept it.

"It is true. We were not friends," she said. "I do not like her because she try to nibble my horse."

"Nibble . . . ? Ah, she tried to nobble your horse. Drug it or something."

"I think so. I pull her away and she try to kick me. I hatted her."

"You hated her."

"No, I hatted her — hit her with my hat." She knocked on the top of the hard riding hat. "Her nose is bleeding and she start screaming like a Marseilles whore. I am sorry if sometimes my English is not so good."

"Your English is *so* much better than my French," Agatha admitted. "Charles speaks excellent French, but mine is pretty much limited to *J'aime la mode française, j'aime la cuisine française, j'aime les vins français* and *j'aime les hommes français.*"

"Ha ha!" laughed Claudette, clapping her hands. "Very good! Where did you learn this?"

"From a waiter at a café in Paris, in Saint-Germain-des-Prés. He said it was all the French an attractive woman ever needed to know."

"But you pronounce it very well for someone who says she speaks no French."

"I'm very good at picking up accents," said Agatha, recalling the effort she had put in to losing her broad Birmingham accent when she first moved to London, and instantly suffering a lightning-fast series of flashbacks to uncomfortable public moments of stress and bad temper when her speech had been overwhelmed by a returning flood of the Brummie twang.

"Ah, Saint-Germain-des-Prés," Claudette sighed. "I have not been there for so long. Not the finest area of Paris to stay, but so much fun, and most exotic. This was where Jean-Paul Sartre and Simone de Beauvoir frequented the cafés. I studied them in college."

"I studied in the cafés," said Agatha. "It was very hot and my room had no air conditioning. I discovered that there were cafés that would stay open as late as you liked, so I sat at a table on the pavement, sipping wine almost until dawn."

An old-fashioned car horn honked outside.

"We had better go," said Agatha. "We don't want to miss our flight."

"We will not miss the flight," Claudette smiled, "but we must go anyway. We will talk more later."

With Claudette in the front passenger seat, her baggage stowed at her feet, Bella thundered out onto the A44, heading south towards Oxford. Before long, a sign announced their arrival at London Oxford Airport, a far more intimate facility than Heathrow, Gatwick or any of the bigger commercial airports surrounding the capital. They passed smoothly through security checks and were shown out of the terminal building onto the runway, where, to Agatha's relief, a modern twin-engined aircraft stood waiting for them. It was not a jet, but neither was it an antique biplane or an airship. The propellers were turning, creating more of a din than Bella had done, and a man wearing overalls and ear protectors loaded their baggage into the hold.

"Where are the other passengers?" Agatha asked Claudette, shouting above the engine noise.

"No others." Claudette shrugged. "This is my uncle's aeroplane — well, our company's aeroplane."

The Colonel had climbed the short flight of steps to the aircraft. He looked back at Agatha, laughed and winked, then ducked in through the door. She smiled. A private plane — another of his little surprises. With Jen and Claudette chatting to one of the ground staff, Agatha approached the steps and was suddenly caught in a blast of air from the propellers. The pleated skirt of her dress shot up into her armpits, leaving her practically naked from the waist down. Hat in one hand, clutch bag in the other, she quickly forced it back down and trotted up the steps into the plane. Why had she not worn trousers for travelling? Nothing to worry about. No one had seen a thing. Inside, the Colonel was standing at the front of the cabin, leaning in through the cockpit door, doubtless talking technical gobbledygook with the pilot. Agatha counted comfortable seats for at least a dozen people. She chose one and buckled herself in. Jen and Claudette joined her, strapping themselves in to two seats facing hers.

"That was a spectacular Marilyn Monroe impression at the foot of the stairs," Jen grinned.

"Just as well you have good legs," added Claudette. Agatha felt her face begin to flush.

"And knickers every bit as nice as the ones poking out of your suitcase!" The two women burst into laughter. Agatha scowled and tensed. She was not used to being teased. In fact, she positively loathed people poking fun at her. Yet here she was, flying in a private plane to Bordeaux with two of the nicest women she had met in a long time. They laughed a lot. They were happy. She felt some of the stress of the past few months beginning to ebb. Relaxing her shoulders, she permitted herself a smile and joined in the laughter. The three of them then talked like old friends for the entire two-hour flight while the Colonel sat several seats away, engrossed in his green-ledger laptop.

Bordeaux airport was a far grander affair than London Oxford. Agatha peered out of her window at the gleaming white control tower and the rooflines of the modern terminal buildings that curved, swooped and soared as though they were ready to take off with the airliners nestling patiently in their allotted berths. She and her travel companions were swiftly processed through

219

the arrivals formalities and headed for the car park, the Colonel steering a trolley piled with their baggage.

"My turn to drive," Claudette announced cheerily, popping open the tailgate of a burgundy Range Rover and helping the Colonel load the bags.

The airport lay to the west of Bordeaux and they avoided the city, Claudette taking a road heading north into the flat plain of the Gironde, the area where the Dordogne and Garonne rivers combined on their long journey to the Bay of Biscay. She did not go that far, driving for around forty minutes, most of which was through endless fields of vines. Unlike the undulating farmland that Agatha was used to in the low hills of the Cotswolds, here the fields ran away from the road as a flat carpet of vines, planted in rows perfectly straight enough to gain even James's seal of approval. Small copses of trees grew here and there, breaking the beautifully geometric monotony of the vines.

Eventually Claudette turned onto a narrow road that led through the vines and into a cluster of trees before emerging into an area of formal lawned gardens, at the centre of which stood a breathtaking chateau.

"Looks amazing, doesn't it?" said Jen, sitting in the back of the car beside Agatha.

"It's like . . . it's like what I would have drawn as my dream castle when I was a little girl," Agatha replied.

"Yes," Jen giggled. "I know exactly what you mean."

The stone walls appeared almost white in the sunshine beneath the roofs of blue-grey slate. Tall pointed roofs topped the round towers at the front of the building, while triangular roofs behind them ran towards the back of the building, flanking the largest section above the central structure. There were three floors of tall, elegant windows and a pair of curving staircases that swept up towards the main entrance. The chateau was not as big as Barfield House, which was good, and a hundred times more beautiful, which was even better. It was not, Agatha realised, a building of any historical significance. It was a fantasy house conjured up by a nineteenth-century architect in a flourish of romantic fervour, built to impress and continuing to achieve that purpose two hundred years later.

"You are in your usual room, of course," Claudette informed Jen and the Colonel, abandoning the car near the staircase. "Come on, Agatha. I will show you your room. Leave the bags. Pierre will bring them. *Bonjour,* Pierre!" She waved to a middle-aged man who was approaching the car. He waved back and smiled. So much more welcoming than Gustav, thought Agatha. So much more relaxed.

Claudette linked her arm through Agatha's. She is so excitable, Agatha mused, so full of life. She still has the youthful exuberance of a child. She has not let the years taint her with cynicism or burden her with the worries of an adult. She's like Peter Pan. Agatha shuddered. She'd always hated Peter Pan. She'd have cut short his crowing far more effectively than Captain Hook. In the meantime, however, Claudette was a breath of fresh air, and Agatha decided to enjoy her company, at least until the air grew stale.

Claudette whisked her on a whirlwind tour of corridors and rooms dripping with ornate cornices and plasterwork, polished doors bordered with elaborate architraves, floors strewn with exquisite rugs, and rooms furnished in the elegant style demanded by a mini palace. Agatha's room was everything she could have expected. She had her own en suite bathroom, a balcony looking out over the vineyards and a giant four-poster bed. Pierre had deposited her suitcase in the room and Agatha freshened up before joining the others on the terrace. There was the pop of a cork and a cheer just as she arrived.

"Champagne," she said. "How lovely."

"Not champagne," Claudette corrected. "Crémant de Bordeaux. As good as most champagne, I think. I do not produce it here, but I like to stay loyal to the area."

They chatted and sipped the sparkling wine in the sunshine before Claudette took Agatha out to view the vines.

"They are just beginning to grow now," she explained. "I will not harvest the grapes until September. This is my part of the business. In different areas I have Cabernet Sauvignon grapes, Merlot and some Cabernet Franc. I even experimented with Petit Verdot, but that ripens too late in the season for me."

"This is a huge area of land," said Agatha, looking out over a sea of vines.

"It is, and very productive," Claudette confirmed. "We shall try a little of the produce at dinner. I have some work to do, but you must relax. You can use the pool if you wish, or just enjoy the sunshine."

Dinner was served on the terrace that evening, when the heat had gone from the sun. Agatha wore a dark-purple cotton dress that she hoped would be appropriate — making an effort without being too showy — and was pleased that Jen, Claudette and the Colonel had also dressed a couple of rungs short of formal evening wear.

Claudette's wine was excellent, the food was delicious and the company was delightful, although the Colonel and Jen took themselves off to bed soon after dinner, ready for an early start in the morning.

"I too have an early start," said Claudette, recharging Agatha's glass and topping up her own, "so this will be my last glass of the evening. We will go to the event together tomorrow morning, yes? Then you can see how it all happens."

"I need to ask," said Agatha, "if you know anyone else who might harbour a grudge against Mary . . . anyone else whose horse she tried to nobble?"

"I think Mary argued with many people, but the only other rider I can think of who caught her in the act was a woman they call Cherry. I do not know her full name. She is not a friend."

"Will she be there tomorrow?"

"I think so. She competes. She has many men who give her money, otherwise, well . . . this life is very expensive, no?"

"Will you be able to point her out to me?"

"Of course, but . . ." Claudette sighed and smiled, wagging a reproachful finger. "I thought for a moment that we had managed to make you relax, Agatha, but you are still on duty, still doing your job."

"It's not just my job," Agatha explained. "I have to find the killer, otherwise there is a very real risk that Charles will be saddled with the blame."

"I have heard of your Sir Charles. They say he is quite handsome."

"He is."

"And they say he is most charming."

"He is."

"And a wonderful lover."

"He . . ." Agatha hesitated, then saw Claudette's cheeky smile.

"Aha, Agatha." She laughed. "He has stolen your heart, no?"

"He did once," Agatha admitted, "but I reclaimed it some time ago. We are just friends."

"This is good," said Claudette, holding her glass aloft. "We should love our friends, and be friends with our lovers!"

Agatha joined in the toast, then finished her drink and made her way to her room, feeling more than a little wine-sleepy and longing for the big four-poster.

CHAPTER EIGHT

Saturday morning dawned bright and clear over the Gironde vineyards. There were early signs of life at the chateau and Agatha heard a car heading off through the vineyard before her eyes were properly open. She blinked, looked up and froze. She was in a box. Why was she sleeping in a box? Then she realised that the box lid was not, in fact, a lid but the canopy over her magnificent four-poster bed.

She stood under the shower, letting the streams of water from the huge circular shower head pummel her body awake, then strolled around the bedroom, towelling herself dry. The room had a high ceiling and she counted fifteen paces to take her from the door of the en suite bathroom to the dressing table on the opposite wall. It was such a luxury to have so much space. I could fit my cottage bedroom into this room at least twice, she thought. Gazing up at the intricate fruit-and-flower plasterwork of the ceiling rose, she decided that she'd probably have space for another two of her own bedrooms up above.

Wrapping her towel into a turban around her wet hair, she flung open the shutters and squinted against the sudden blaze of sunlight. Stepping to the left, she stood in front of a full-length mirror and cast a critical eye over herself. There's no escaping it, she told herself, I have the body of a middle-aged woman. She smoothed her hands over her neck to pull the skin tight, then prodded herself in the waist. It was getting thicker, but there was still hope. Turning slightly to the side, she pushed her shoulders back, sucked her stomach in and stretched one leg slightly forward, the way models did in the fashion pages. That's better, she thought. Mind you, I can't stand around stark naked all day at a gymkhana. So what am I going to wear?

She heard the clink of coffee cups from the terrace and the sound of Claudette and Jen laughing. Do they never stop laughing? she wondered. Surely it's far too early in the morning for that? Only those maniacs on radio breakfast shows laugh this early, and I can switch them off. How can I decide what to wear with them howling away?

Hang on . . . I wonder what *they're* wearing.

She looked towards the open balcony doors and the stone balustrade beyond. Dropping to her hands and knees, she crawled out onto the balcony and peeked over the balustrade down to the left. Claudette had her hair pulled back into a ponytail. She was wearing a white blouse, cream jodhpurs and gleaming black riding boots. She looked fantastic, but that was no help at all to Agatha. Claudette was a competitor and Agatha would be a mere spectator. Jen was better. A simple floral dress, elegant and summery. That was more like it.

"Morning, Agatha!"

The Colonel strode past below on the right. Agatha squeezed her eyes shut tight, as if to make him disappear, then gave a little wave and quickly crawled backwards into the bedroom. How much did he see? No matter. The Colonel was a gentleman. He wouldn't say anything. A burst of laughter echoed up from the terrace. Gentleman my arse!

Agatha dried her hair at the dressing table, applied her make-up, then retrieved a yellow linen shift dress from the bathroom. Linen had a tendency to crumple, but the dress had survived being packed in the suitcase reasonably well. The steamy bath-room had helped to disperse any slight creases. She had picked it off a rack in one of her favourite Mircester stores because she liked the look of the V neck and the cap sleeves. She had almost put it back when the tag described it as perfect for "apple-shaped women." Agatha was not prepared to admit that she was apple-shaped, but the darts below the bust cinched the waist slightly, allowing the dress to hang so well on her when she tried it, the hemline just above the knee, that she couldn't resist it. She held it against herself and checked it in the mirror. It would be perfect for today. She dressed quickly and joined the others on the terrace for a light breakfast.

Claudette drove them all to the event in her Range Rover. They headed towards the Bay of Biscay coast, where they arrived at a showground that was already buzzing with activity. A queue of cars tailed back from the entrance onto the main road, but Clau-dette turned towards a side gate, the competitors' entrance, where there was no queue. She showed a pass and was waved through after a friendly chat.

"We have a good spot," she said. "I was here with the Colonel earlier this morning. I talked to Pierre and to Poppy, my horse.

She is in good shape. I am hoping for a good result today!"

"We'll be cheering you on, won't we, Agatha?" said Jen.

"Of course," said Agatha. "Good heavens — this place is enormous!"

The showground was a vast flat area with two large white-painted grandstands looking out over competition arenas. The flags of many nations fluttered weakly in a whisper of breeze. Scores of spectators strolled along avenues of parked cars, exchanging lively greetings with others picnicking under open tailgates. There were vans where food vendors offered crêpes and ice creams, marquees where corporate sponsors were entertaining important clients, and event marshals patrolling in high-visibility green jackets. The whole place was buzzing with activity.

"Exciting, isn't it?" said Jen, patting Agatha's thigh. "You're going to love this — we'll have a gorgeous lunch later. This is such a fun day out!"

"Our area is just over there," said Claudette, steering the car past a knot of people. "I don't like to drive the horse transporter. Too big for me. Pierre has everything ready."

Claudette showed her pass at the entrance to the competitors' enclosure and the nature of the parked vehicles changed from everyday cars to horse boxes, four-wheel drives of every variety and horse transporters the size of commercial trucks. Claudette pulled in beside one of the gargantuan transporters, which was patriotically painted in the red, white and blue of the French tricolour. Pierre was there waiting for them. He handed a sheaf of papers to Claudette. The Colonel disappeared to attend to official duties.

"There is paperwork — formalities." Claudette smiled, handing Agatha and Jen lanyards with credit-card-sized passes. "Your jewellery for today." She laughed. "It will not suit your dress, Agatha, but you must not lose it. Okay, I must go."

"Where might I find the woman you mentioned?" Agatha asked. "The woman called Cherry?"

"I think she has the big silver transporter down there," said Claudette, pointing. "She will not be there right now. You should try later. Now I must go to see Poppy."

Claudette hurried off and Jen suggested that she and Agatha take a stroll to find their bearings. They walked past dozens of transporters, some with horses hanging their heads out of open windows, eyeing them curiously. Everywhere, with no wind to disperse it, the scent of horses hung ripe in the air. In some places the smell was so thick you could almost taste it. Agatha held her nose. Jen giggled.

"You get used to it after a while," she said. "Come on, let's see where Claudette will be riding."

They found the show-jumping arena in front of one of the white grandstands. A contest for juvenile riders was under way. Children, faces set in grim concentration, pounded the sandy surface of the course on ponies that flew over brush-hedge fences, red-and-white-painted gates and walls made from hollow plywood bricks. Like the wooden bars of the gates and fences, the bricks were intended to be knocked over if the horse hit the obstacle. Agatha saw a number of fences collapse and several walls destroyed. There were tears from the losers, jubilation and rosettes for the winners, cheers and applause for everyone.

Back at the transporter, Claudette had returned and was sipping a coffee.

"Everything is ready," she said, sounding nervous. "I ride shortly. Agatha, I have seen Cherry and her friends at her transporter."

"Thank you," said Agatha. "I will try to have a quick word with her now."

Leaving Jen quietly soothing Claudette's

nerves, Agatha wandered off in the direction of the silver transporter. It stood in a line of vehicles, their backs towards a sheltering thicket of trees. There were no signs of life at the front, but a strong, handsome black horse stood calmly at the side, tethered in the shade. Female English voices in lively conversation came from the rear. Agatha approached the open tailgate. Three women were inside the transporter. Two were casually dressed, one leaning against a saddle slung over a low trestle and one passing a silver hip flask to the third, who was the only one in the competition uniform of boots, jodhpurs and jacket. She had her back to the tailgate.

"What do you want?" called one of the women, spotting Agatha.

"I'm looking for Cherry . . ." Agatha replied, then stopped as the figure in the black jacket turned to face her. Her blonde hair was pulled back into a tight bun and her make-up was, Agatha judged, a trifle heavy, but immaculate. She had a familiar thin smile on her face and an even more familiar jewelled horse brooch on her jacket.

"So, not Cherry," said Agatha. "Sherry — Sheraton Chadwick."

"Agatha Raisin," said Chadwick. "I've been wondering when you might turn up. I

233

wasn't expecting you here, though."

"Oh, I'm full of surprises," said Agatha.

"Come in," Chadwick invited, offering the hip flask. "Have a drink."

"Not for me, thanks," said Agatha, stepping into the transporter. "I was hoping to have a word with you about —"

"Her Royal Highness Queen Mary Darlinda Brown-Field Fraith, deceased." Chadwick smirked. "You've been making a nuisance of yourself pestering everyone about her, haven't you?"

"It's important that I —"

"It's not important. Mary wasn't important. You're not important — so nothing that you do is important, Mrs. Private Detective."

"Is this her?" one of the other women snorted. "Is this the private eye? Not much to look at, is she?"

Agatha shot her a look. "You must have been born at home," she said. "That's where most accidents happen."

"Ha!" laughed the third woman. "Mary must definitely have been born at home, then!" She stuck out her chin and waggled her head, in a crude impersonation. "It's *Lady Mary* to you! It's *Lady Mary* to you!"

The other two shrieked with laughter. Agatha scowled at Sheraton Chadwick.

"You wouldn't be so quick to mock her father, would you, Mrs. Chadwick? Nice brooch, by the way. I think I can hazard a guess where that came from."

"Have you been spying on me, Mrs. Raisin? I really don't like snoopers, you know."

"Oh, I know all about what you like," said Agatha, nodding towards the saddle. "Is that all ready for you to 'Saddle Up the Palomino'? "

"I think we need to teach you a lesson, you old cow!"

Sheraton Chadwick made a grab for Agatha, who dodged aside, only for one of the other women to reach out and seize her arm.

"Snakes and bastards!" she hissed. Following Claudette's example, she grabbed a riding helmet hanging on the transporter wall and smashed it into the face of her captor. The woman staggered back, holding her nose. Agatha lunged towards the tailgate. Chadwick stepped in front of her and the uninjured woman leapt on her from behind. Agatha squirmed, kicked and twisted, but now the woman she had hit was there again and the two held her fast.

Chadwick stepped towards her. She held a leather riding crop in her hand and pressed the tip under Agatha's chin. Agatha tried to break away, but her arms were twisted and tightly gripped by Chadwick's friends.

"When I caught the lovely Mary in here," Chadwick snarled, "I gave her a taste of this." She shoved the riding crop harder into Agatha's throat. "Now you've hurt my friend Charlotte. You will have to be punished."

She stepped back and pointed to the saddle. Her friends bent Agatha's arms behind her back and she was thrust forward, crashing into the saddle and collapsing over it, her assailants maintaining their ferocious and painful grip. She was bent double, her face just inches from the straw on the floor, her hair falling into her face as she fought to straighten up, but Charlotte was standing over her, pinning her arms behind her and pushing her down. The other woman quickly locked her arms around Agatha's ankles, clamping them together and pulling her feet clear of the floor. Now Agatha could barely move, barely breathe. She felt her dress being yanked up to her buttocks. Chadwick laid the riding crop across the top of her thighs.

"Your sweet little summer dress isn't going to look nearly so pretty when you've a lovely set of tiger stripes down the backs of your legs, is it?" she purred. "You've been a very naughty pony . . ."

"STOP THAT! Let her go!"

Agatha recognised Jen's voice, but not the tone. She had never heard Jen angry. She felt her legs being released and her feet hit the floor. Then her arms were free. She eased them down to her sides, pushing away from the saddle to stand up. She smoothed her dress and pushed her hair out of her face.

"You people are *animals*!" Jen was standing at the tailgate. Pierre's strong hand was clamped around Chadwick's wrist. He took the riding crop and pushed her aside.

"Thank you, Jen," said Agatha, regaining her composure. She picked up her clutch bag, dropped during the struggle, and, spotting a small mirror on the wall, ran her fingers through her hair and checked her make-up. She turned to Charlotte, offering her a tissue to mop up the blood dribbling from her nose. "Poor Charlotte," she said. "I'd like to say I'm sorry . . . but I'm not." Then she faced Sheraton Chadwick, fixing her with her bear-like eyes. "This isn't over," she growled.

"You don't frighten me," Chadwick sneered. "I can buy and sell low-life like you. Cross me again, and you're dead!"

"A threat?" said Agatha, shaking her head. "Oh dear. Big mistake. You really don't know me at all, do you?"

She strode out of the trailer with Jen at her side. Pierre followed quietly behind.

"Are you all right, Agatha?" asked Jen once they were well away from Chadwick's transporter.

"I'm fine," said Agatha, turning her face to the sun and breathing deeply. "A little shaken, maybe, but nothing a good stiff drink can't put right."

"That's the spirit," said Jen. "There's a bar at the grandstand. Claudette will be riding shortly, so let's go there. What on earth were you doing with that lot?"

"I was doing my job. Sometimes it can get a little rough."

"Well, Sheraton Chadwick is no stranger to that sort of thing, I can tell you. She once took a riding crop to a young girl who only wanted to stroke her horse. I'm sorry you ran into someone like her here. She is not typical of the sort of people we know on the circuit. Most are extremely nice. She, on the other hand, is a particularly nasty piece of work."

"So it seems. I have a . . . professional interest in her."

"Be very careful with that one, Agatha.

She's ruthless. No morals. She uses her husband's money to finance her riding jaunts, and when he reins in the cash from time to time, she simply turns to another benefactor. I could name at least three men, in Italy, Germany and the Netherlands, whose bed she shares when she needs an injection of corporate finance."

"Is that so?" Agatha said quietly. "Jen, I may have to press you for those names later. I will make each one a nail in Sheraton Chadwick's coffin. In the meantime, let's go get that drink."

By the time they had reached the grandstand and picked up two glasses of deliciously cold white wine from the bar, the show-jumping was already under way. They took their seats to watch the rider preceding Claudette finish her round. Even a novice like Agatha could tell that the jumps for the adult contest were higher, and there were more of them, spread out over a longer course. The rider guided her horse with great skill, but at the final jump one of her horse's rear hooves clipped the wall, sending a couple of bricks toppling to the ground. There was a groan of disappointment from the crowd but cheers and applause nonetheless when she finished the course.

Claudette was in the arena next with Poppy. She looked lean and athletic balanced on the powerful grey mare, tackling the course with confidence. Agatha noticed Jen rising and falling in the seat next to her, taking every jump and turn along with her friend. Horse and rider moved in smooth harmony, tension and expectation building in the crowd until Claudette faced the final wall. Poppy surged forward and took a mighty leap, sailing well clear of the top. There was a huge roar and a thunder of applause from the crowd. Jen and Agatha were on their feet cheering, Agatha totally caught up in the excitement of the moment.

"Come on," said Jen. "Let's go and have a word with her!"

They rushed down the stairs from the grandstand to find Claudette in a small paddock with Poppy, Pierre in attendance. She was jumping up and down in elation. Other competitors were milling around, congratulating her on a fine performance. Jen hugged her, and Claudette hugged Agatha, squealing with excitement.

"Does that mean you've won?" Agatha asked.

"Not quite," Claudette grinned, "but it was a very good start. Poppy was fantastic, no? There is more to do, but that was a clear round in a fast time. Our best performance, I think. Whatever else happens today, tonight we will celebrate at dinner in a restaurant close to the chateau. You will love it."

"We'd best stick to a light lunch, then, Agatha!" Jen laughed. "We'll watch Claudette ride again later."

"I can't wait," said Agatha. Then, as Claudette chatted happily with friends, she said quietly to Jen and Pierre, "Say nothing about that little incident earlier. We don't want to spoil Claudette's day in any way. I will deal with Sheraton Chadwick."

Agatha sat at the dressing table in her room at the chateau. She had showered and changed and was putting the finishing touches to her make-up, with the events of the day running through her head. Claudette and Poppy had enjoyed a triumphantly successful day and were well placed for the next stage of the competition tomorrow. The time Agatha had spent with Jen had been a delight . . . but then there was Sheraton Chadwick.

She shuddered. The truth was that she had thought of little else all day. Whenever there were no other distractions, when there was nothing else to occupy her mind, or even when she drifted momentarily out of a conversation, snatches of the confrontation played out in her head. Every time it happened, she felt a surge of anger. She had been humiliated. She had been frightened. She had been very frightened when they draped her over that saddle, waiting for the hot, sharp sting of the riding crop on the backs of her legs. If Jen hadn't come looking for her . . . She gulped a breath of air. A tear forced its way out of the corner of her eye. She dabbed at it with a tissue. Thank God for waterproof mascara! She gave herself a shake. This will *not* do, she told herself. She was *not* going to be upset. She was going to enjoy an evening with friends. Sheraton Chadwick would get what was coming to her.

She checked herself in the full-length mirror before going downstairs. The black sequinned dress was mid length and the neckline respectable rather than daringly low. It was a cocktail dress as opposed to an evening gown — ideal for an early dinner at any restaurant. The temperature was markedly cooler, a change in the weather clearly on the way, so she draped a silver-flecked black pashmina over her shoulders. She was ready.

Downstairs in the lounge, Claudette and Jen were sipping glasses of Crémant with the Colonel, who had his ledger laptop open on a table.

"Just in time, Agatha my dear!" he called, holding out a glass of sparkling wine for her. "Come and take a look at this!"

A video was playing on the laptop. Agatha could see the show-jumping arena and glimpses of the crowd, then the camera was racing towards one of the jumps and soaring over it, Poppy's neck and ears filling part of the screen. There was the sound of pounding hooves, Poppy snorting and Claudette breathing words of encouragement. It was a record of the day's success, all from Claudette's point of view.

"Amazing," said Agatha. "How on earth did you do that?"

"With one of these," said the Colonel, holding out a handful of what looked like colourful buttons. "These little beauties can transmit video and sound direct to my laptop. Decent-quality results and they weigh next to nothing."

"Good evening," came a voice from the doorway. "I hope I am not missing anything."

A man stood in the doorway, looking directly at Agatha. He was of medium height with strong, broad shoulders and smouldering dark eyes.

"Uncle Pascal!" Claudette threw her arms around his neck and kissed him. "You made it!"

"A little late, and I must leave again for London tomorrow." He smiled and shrugged. "But tonight I shall have dinner with my beautiful niece, our wonderful friends and . . . a charming lady."

Claudette introduced her uncle to Agatha. She went to shake his hand, but he took hers, lifted it to his lips and kissed it.

"Delighted to meet you, Agatha," he said. "We must talk later. I want to know all about you."

"I . . . well, yes . . . of course," Agatha felt her face flush slightly. Agatha Raisin! she scolded herself. Get a grip! You're behaving like a silly little girl . . . but, well, he is devilishly handsome . . .

Claudette drove to the restaurant. She would have only one glass of wine, she declared, because she needed to keep a clear head for the dressage competition the following day. This was also the reason they were eating early. Both Claudette and the Colonel had to be up early the next morning to get back to the showground. Because Agatha wanted to get home for work, it had been decided that she would fly to Oxford with Pascal.

The restaurant reminded her of a number of Cotswold inns. It was centuries old, sitting at a crossroads in the heart of the countryside just a few minutes' drive from the chateau. Inside, there were low ceilings with wooden beams, subdued lighting and a maze of discreet nooks and crannies where the chic tables looked intimately inviting. She surprised herself by suddenly imagining James beckoning her to sit at one of the tables. She had visited far more places like this with Charles than she ever had with James, yet it was James who had sprung to mind. He would, she decided, appreciate the atmosphere here far more than Charles, and would probably include it in one of his travel articles.

They enjoyed a sumptuous meal and a choice of wines with each course, Pascal insisting on explaining to Agatha the intricacies of each distinct variety. He chatted to her about Paris, London and bizarre and amusing experiences of corporate life. Agatha relished the atmosphere, the conversation and the wine, but paused as she was about to sample the final vintage of the evening. From where she was sitting, she had a view across the restaurant, now busy with clients. Standing at the door, being attended to by the maître d', was Darell

Brown-Field with Mrs. Sheraton Chadwick on his arm. Agatha reached into her handbag, grabbed her phone and snapped a photo. Neither Brown-Field nor Chadwick noticed a thing, and they were shown to a table out of sight on the far side of the restaurant without spotting her. They must have thought they were safe here, she smiled, miles from anywhere in the heart of the French countryside at a restaurant where no one would know them. Now, whatever they chose for dinner, their goose was cooked.

"You wish to take a photo?" asked Pascal.

"Just that one," Agatha replied. "I wanted to capture . . . the ambience."

Back at the chateau, Agatha and Pascal lingered in the drawing room, chatting merrily over balloons of cognac long after the others had gone to bed. When Agatha decided that she too needed to turn in, he took her arm and linked it into his own as they walked towards the stairs.

"It seems such a shame to part now simply to be together again so early in the morning," he said. He bent his head towards her and kissed her on the lips. For a second, she let him, then she placed a hand on his chest and pushed herself gently out of his embrace.

"I'm sorry," she said. "I have had such fun with you tonight, but I don't feel quite ready for . . ."

"As you wish," he replied softly. "I apologise if I have upset you in any way."

"Not at all. No apology necessary, Pascal, really. I will see you in the morning. Goodnight."

Agatha trotted upstairs to her room and threw herself on the bed. Pascal had been utterly charming and he simply oozed sex appeal. After such a wonderful evening, how could she resist such a gorgeous Frenchman, with his velvety smooth accent, who seemed totally besotted with her, in a fairytale castle? Because, Agatha Raisin, she told herself, your life is complicated enough right now. What about James? How could you start leading him to think that you could be together again when you're not at all sure about it yourself? How could you kiss a Frenchman who is practically a stranger if what you really want is a life with James? How could you get yourself confused about all of this that is so incompatible with . . . and before she could work out exactly what it was not compatible with, she was sound asleep.

Having woken in the middle of the night

247

with the shoulder of her dress pressing fish-scale sequin patterns into the side of her face, Agatha was not entirely ready to face the day by the time she was due to leave for the airport with Pascal. He understood entirely that sensible conversation would be delayed until the head fog of the night before had cleared, and spent most of the journey studying the financial section of his newspaper or sifting through papers from his briefcase.

By the time they were airborne and Agatha was sipping her fourth cup of coffee of the morning, they were able to resume their amiable conversation from the night before, and when they parted in the terminal building in Oxford, she knew that she wanted to see him again, though she needed to have her life back on the rails before then.

"You have a car here at the airport?" he asked.

"No, Toni will pick me up."

"He is a good friend, your Tony?"

"He is a she," Agatha laughed, "but yes — a good friend and colleague. Toni works for me."

There was a short pause as she tried to find her next words.

"Pascal, last night I was a little . . ."

He waved a hand to dismiss any awkward

thoughts, as though pushing them aside.

"I was too forward," he said, "too eager. You must allow me to make it up to you. You must visit us at the chateau again soon. From tomorrow, I will be spending the next month there. Every day. Promise me you will come."

"I promise. As soon as the case is wrapped up, I will come."

"Just phone myself or Claudette to let us know. I will be most delighted to see you again. I am sure Claudette will too, but not, I think, as much as me."

They hugged, then he kissed her on both cheeks and hurried off to talk to the pilot of the plane.

Toni was waiting for Agatha when she came through the arrivals gate.

"Welcome home," she said, smiling. "Good holiday?"

"It was a work trip, my girl," said Agatha, then laughed. "Want to see my holiday snaps? Take this for a second."

She handed Toni her suitcase, pulled out her phone and, still walking towards the car park, held up the image of Darell Brown-Field with Sheraton Chadwick for Toni to admire.

"Wow!" said Toni. "You got them! Where was that taken?"

"At a restaurant in the Gironde. Come on, I'll fill you in on the rest in the car."

As they headed north up the A44, Agatha gave Toni an account of her whirlwind trip to Bordeaux, including her experience with Sheraton Chadwick and her friends.

"She is one sick, nasty bitch," Toni gasped. "Would she really have flogged you with that thing?"

"If Jen hadn't shown up with Pierre, I'm certain she would. She's capable of just about anything."

"How about murder?"

"No doubt about it."

"But what motive would she have for killing Mary?"

"I've been puzzling over that most of the way home. Clearly she wanted to squeeze as much cash out of Darell as she could. Murdering his daughter wouldn't help her in that respect. I suppose Mary could have been blackmailing her about the affair with her father, or about her other lovers. I have the names of three of them."

"I suppose that at least puts the Chadwick case to bed, so to speak. We have everything we need to report back to Mr. Chadwick on what his wife's been up to."

"Not just Mr. Chadwick. I'm going to make sure the whole world knows what a money-grabbing whore she is."

There was an uncomfortable silence as Agatha nursed her wrath. A few spots of rain spattered the windscreen and the wipers noisily scraped them away.

"News on Deborah Lexington," said Toni eventually. "Simon and I have been in touch with every medical centre and nursing agency in the area. Simon knows a couple of nurses . . . quite a few actually . . . but a couple who had colleagues who used to visit Deborah Lexington at home. They haven't been to see her for at least three months and we can't find any evidence that she is receiving ongoing medical care. Remember the young doctor I was seeing?"

"Oh, don't tell me you're back with him again!" Agatha sighed. She hated it when Toni got herself tangled up in a relationship. She wasn't nearly as useful at work and Agatha always ended up falling out with her. The doctor had been the worst.

"No, I'm not, but why would it be such a . . ." Toni shook her head, determined not to be sidetracked by a hostile debate with Agatha about her love life. "Anyway, he said that he knew someone involved with Deborah's treatment and couldn't believe that she hadn't fully recovered."

"Interesting . . ." Agatha fished out her

phone and hit a speed-dial number. "Simon? Yes, I'm back. Yes, I know it's a Sunday. No, I don't want you to stake out the Chadwick house. I need you to stake out the Lexington house instead. Yes, tonight. Toni will send you the address shortly. Good. Let's talk again tomorrow."

Toni dropped Agatha at her cottage in Lilac Lane. Agatha shivered as she hauled her suitcase out of the car. It was far cooler than when she had left. She would have to exchange her summer frocks for something more substantial. She dropped the suitcase in the hall and looked towards the kitchen. No cats came scampering. When she walked into her living room, she realised why. Roy was stretched out on the sofa, watching TV with both of them curled up in his lap.

"I thought you said they didn't like you?" she said.

"I've been the one feeding them, darling," Roy replied. "They worship the giver of food."

"How are your legs?"

"Better, but worse. They were *so* much worse yesterday. Tamara warned me that the stiffness would be worst a couple of days after I started. The only way to make it bearable is to carry on riding. Who'd have thought that the cure for the agony of exercise was to take more of the exercise that caused the agony in the first place? Now I can't feel the old pain for the new pain."

"Still hooked on riding?"

"Absolutely. I am bravely suffering and still hooked. Tamara says I'll soon be ready to try a rising trot."

"Good. I need you to keep poking around at the stables."

"That car has been back again overnight — the boyfriend's car."

Agatha crossed the room to her drinks cabinet, decided against a gin and tonic now that the weather had turned, and poured herself a whisky. She offered one to Roy.

"What sort of car is it?" she asked.

"A red Ford hatchback."

"Really? That's the same as the Lexingtons' car."

"Surely just a coincidence, darling," said Roy, deciding he was bored with the cookery programme he had been watching. The likelihood of him ever poaching a whole octopus was fairly remote. "There must be thousands of red Fords around."

"I don't believe in coincidences in a murder investigation. Did you get the registration?"

Roy rattled off the number he had memorised from the car's licence plate and took a sip of his drink, watching while Agatha tapped an icon on her phone.

"You're already there? Well done, Simon. Is the red car in the driveway? What's the licence number? Thank you."

Agatha slowly placed her phone on a side table and sat down in an armchair. She sampled her whisky and looked over at Roy.

"Very interesting," she mused. "Jacob Lexington has been calling on Tamara Montgomery."

CHAPTER NINE

Roy Silver reckoned that he had worked out at least seven new ways to walk. It all depended on which bit of him was hurting most. His gait had gone from his usual casual London amble, occasionally quickened with a spirit of urgency when he wanted to demonstrate serious intent, to a cowboy roll, then a drunk-type stagger, then something totally alien that he could only liken to a sparrow attempting to lay an ostrich egg. When he walked into the tack room at Montgomery Stables that morning, he was cruising in cowboy mode.

He was carrying various items of kit that had to be cleaned and put back in their allotted places. Roy was not a naturally tidy person himself, but he respected the way Tamara kept everything in order. Nothing was ever lost or mislaid, which meant that anything you needed for dealing with the horses was always to hand. He was surprised to see the lid of the blanket box sitting slightly open and the corner of a grey padded horse blanket poking out. That was not the way things were usually left around here.

As he lifted the lid to tuck the blanket back inside, he spotted some shimmering gold material farther down in the box. That surely had no place with the blankets. He lifted a couple of blankets aside and frowned. Something was very wrong. He reached a hand into his pocket for his phone.

At the Raisin Investigations office, Agatha was perched on the edge of Toni's desk with a mug of coffee. Having done the Lexington night shift, Simon was at home, and Patrick was also absent, having taken over the surveillance. Helen Freedman was filing papers in a cabinet drawer and Toni sat with her hands cupped around her own coffee mug.

"Jacob Lexington and Tamara Montgomery?" she said. "Really?"

"Really." Agatha nodded.

"They don't seem a likely couple."

"Things ain't always —"

There was a drumbeat of footsteps coming up the stairs and the office door crashed open. Darell Brown-Field stomped in, eyes blazing with fury and chin, as always, set like a snow plough.

"You!" he barked, pointing at Agatha. "I want a word with you!"

"Do you have an appointment?" Agatha asked, calmly sipping her coffee. "I'm a bit busy at the moment."

"Don't get mouthy with me, you jumped-up slut!" he yelled. "I know what you've been up to!"

"You know nothing. You're an idiot."

"You stay out of my affairs!"

"You're having more than one, then? Where did you find *two* women with such bad taste?"

"I'm warning you, I —"

"It's all getting a bit loud in here, isn't it?" said Roy Silver, walking in through the open door.

Darell glanced round nervously. Roy was a far from imposing figure, especially in his jodhpurs and riding boots, but Darell clearly felt the odds were now stacked too heavily against him. He turned to leave, giving Agatha a look of pure malice.

"Just you keep your nose out!" he bawled.

"And you keep your chin up," said Agatha.

He thundered down the stairs and slammed the street door.

"What's got him in such a state?" asked Roy.

"Maybe French food doesn't agree with him," said Agatha. "More to the point, what are you doing here? Why aren't you at the stables?"

"There's something you should see," said Roy. He flicked through his phone until a photograph appeared on the screen. "I couldn't send this from the stables. Signal wasn't good enough."

Agatha and Toni looked at the photo. It was of an outfit laid out on a table in the tack room: a long coat embroidered with a gold and silver design, a lacy white shirt, knee breeches and white stockings.

"That looks like an outfit from the masked ball." Agatha frowned.

"Don't you recognise it?" said Toni. "It looks a bit different like this, but I swear we both danced with that costume. It's the one the bloke who first asked you to dance was wearing."

"You're right," Agatha agreed.

"I guessed it was important," said Roy, "but what was it doing hidden in a blanket box at Montgomery Stables?"

"What indeed?" puzzled Agatha.

"Could Tamara have worn it?" Toni wondered. "Maybe she passed herself off as a man to sneak into the party?"

"But we danced with whoever was wearing this," Agatha reasoned. "Whoever it was didn't dance particularly well, but we would have known if it wasn't a bloke."

"What did you do with the costume, Roy?" asked Toni.

"I put it back where I found it," said Roy, "but not as I found it. A blanket hanging out of the box led me to it, which makes me think that it wasn't Tamara who hid the costume there. She does everything too neatly for that."

"So why would anyone hide it in a messy way, in a tidy room?" Agatha wondered. "You were meant to find this, Roy. It was planted there."

"By Jacob Lexington?" said Toni.

"That's who my money's on," Agatha agreed. "Toni, I think you and I need to plan another visit to the Lexingtons. Roy, you had best get back to the stables."

"Okay," said Roy, turning quietly to go. He had hoped for a small pat on the back at the very least for having turned up such an important clue. He cowboy-waddled towards the door.

"Oh, and Roy . . ." Agatha called after him.

"Yes?" he answered, expectantly.

"Hi-ho, Silver!"

Agatha spent the rest of the morning researching the names that Jen Warbler-Dow
had given her — the Italian, the Dutchman
and the German. They were not difficult to
find online. Each was a successful business-
man. Each was extremely rich. Each had
been photographed at glamorous events
with his glamorous wife. Why on earth
would they risk everything for a woman like
Sheraton Chadwick? She wondered if the
men knew each other. It seemed likely,
given that they were all involved with show-
jumping, but Agatha was willing to bet that
they were not close friends. She was also
convinced that none of them was aware that
the others were indulging themselves with
Chadwick. These were not the sort of men
who would want to share. Chadwick was
playing a dangerous game.

As a high-flying PR consultant in London,
Agatha had met many rich, powerful men.
Their egos knew no bounds. They would
revel in the idea that friends and business
associates knew, or suspected, that they were
having an affair. They would think that
made everyone admire their machismo. It
pumped their muscles. Sharing was not part
of the image. Sharing meant they were not

dominant, not top of the tree. That everyone might think they were sharing some English slapper with a couple of other witless cretins would wound them deeply. They could not tolerate the ridicule that would ensue. And the glamorous wives would suddenly acquire expensive lawyers. That would wound them even more deeply. That would be a real pain in the bank account, and Sheraton Chadwick would surely be the one at whom they lashed out. Agatha wondered for a moment if she really wanted to drop Chadwick into that particular arena. Then she thought of being forced over the saddle in the transporter, and that did it. As soon as Agatha was ready, Sheraton Chadwick was being thrown to the lions.

Agatha arranged to meet up with Toni later that afternoon, when Simon was back on shift, to pay another visit to the Lexingtons. Toni had been researching the sale of the Lexingtons' home and CPD Developments, the company that had bought it. Agatha decided to take a look at the CPD notes later and headed off to do a spot of shopping. She ended up back home in Carsely, in Harvey's, the village store, where she was busy clearing the freezer section of individual frozen lasagne portions when she bumped into Margaret Bloxby.

"Agatha, you're back," said Mrs. Bloxby. "I heard you'd gone away for a few days."

"Just a couple of days," Agatha replied. "It was a work thing . . . mainly."

"Mainly? A little pleasure thrown in, I hope?"

"Pleasure? A pleasant time, yes, but also . . . confusion."

"Sounds frustrating. How about a cup of tea?"

"You're on," said Agatha, and, having paid for their shopping, they made their way out onto the high street.

"Oh, sod the tea," said Agatha, looking towards the Red Lion's pub sign. "How about a drink instead? Do vicars' wives frequent pubs?"

"I'm sure I don't know," Mrs. Bloxby replied. "I may be struck down by a bolt of lightning as soon as I cross the threshold."

No sooner had they walked into the pub than the barman called out from behind the beer pumps, "The usual, Margaret?"

"The usual, John," Mrs. Bloxby replied, smiling at Agatha, enjoying her little joke, "and the same for Mrs. Raisin!"

Two glasses of sherry were duly delivered to their table. They clinked glasses and Agatha chatted about everything that had happened on her trip to Bordeaux, focusing mainly on her brief encounter with the sultry Pascal.

"Well," said Mrs. Bloxby, feigning a swoon and fanning herself with a beer mat, "Pascal sounds like quite a man. I don't know if I could have been as strong-willed as you under those circumstances."

"You're teasing," said Agatha, sounding cross. "I thought I could rely on you to —"

"You can, Agatha," Mrs. Bloxby reassured her, laying a calming hand on Agatha's arm. "My point is that not everyone would have stayed true to themselves the way you did."

"And what about staying true to James?"

"James may be part of staying true to yourself. The only advice I can give you is be honest and follow your heart."

"I've followed that up plenty of blind alleys in the past."

"Yet proved yourself to be a loyal companion in the process. You are still, after all, fighting Sir Charles's corner."

"Oh, I wish I could go back to being the old Agatha — the one who built a successful business in cut-throat London and didn't give a stuff about anyone else."

"The old Agatha? The one who demanded promises about her staff's job security before she sold the business and then went bananas when the new owner reneged on that part of the deal?"

"We've talked a lot since I came to Carsely, haven't we?"

"We've got through a lot of sherry."

"But the staff thing was all about me. It was all about me not wanting anyone to think that I had lost out on a deal. I didn't care two hoots about the staff."

"Yet one of them, Roy, still comes to see you, still takes every opportunity to work with you."

"I'm really not as nice as you think I am."

"Or as terrible as *you* think you are. There are people you care about, and those who care about you."

Mrs. Bloxby drained the last drops from her glass. "I must be getting back to the vicarage," she said. "I'm playing meditative piano mood music for the ladies' choral society Pilates class in half an hour."

They gathered their shopping bags and made for the door. Agatha was first to bustle out into the street, bumping straight into a figure walking past.

"Why don't you watch where the hell you're going?" she snarled. "Haven't you got — James!"

"Sorry, Aggie," he apologised with a grin. "Here, let me take those for you."

He stooped to take her bags and Mrs.

Bloxby bade them farewell, heading off to the vicarage and ladies in leotards while they made for Lilac Lane.

"How was Bordeaux?" he asked.

"There were bits you would really have enjoyed," Agatha assured him. "I was thinking about you rather a lot."

"That's nice to know. I —"

"Hey, you! Raisin!" A voice came from a parked car — a red Ford. Jacob Lexington stepped out. "I tried to be nice to you before and that didn't work, so now I'm telling you straight. I know you've had someone watching our house. Call him off. Stay away from us."

"This is getting to be a habit," Agatha muttered to James. "Second one today."

"Don't start any of your smart talk. Just keep your stupid nose out of our business, you old tart."

"I won't have you talking to Agatha like that!" said James, setting down the shopping and stepping towards Jacob.

"Stay out of this, old man!" snarled Jacob, grabbing James to push him aside. The pair took hold of one another and shuffled this way and that, grunting and huffing. No punches were being thrown. No damage was being done. Agatha was beginning to think it wasn't much of a fight and that she probably needed to join in when somebody brushed past her and forced himself between the two men.

"Mircester Police! Calm down, both of you!" It was Bill Wong. "You all right?" he said to James, who nodded and straightened his jacket. Bill turned to Jacob. "Make yourself scarce. I don't want to see you around here again."

Jacob jumped into his car and drove off.

"What was all that about?" Bill asked.

"Mary Brown-Field, what else?" said Agatha.

"That's what I need to talk to you about too," said Bill. "Let's go inside. Quickly, we don't have much time."

James and Bill sat at Agatha's kitchen table while she emptied her shopping bag into her freezer.

"Agatha," said Bill, "Sir Charles has been re-arrested for his wife's murder."

"What?" Agatha scoffed. "On what grounds?"

"New evidence." Bill slipped a sheet of paper out of his pocket and unfolded it on the table. "I shouldn't be showing you this. I shouldn't even be here, but something very fishy is going on and I'm worried that Wilkes is going to find a way to make this stick. This is an email that was retrieved from Sir Charles's computer. It was sent over two months ago, before he married Mary Brown-Field, while they were still engaged. The address it was sent to was somewhere in eastern Europe, but that account could have been handled from anywhere in the world and has since been shut down. There's no way to trace the recipient."

The email message was short and straightforward.

Okay — I'll pay it. It has to happen after the mariage.
I need her off my back. She's driving me crazy. I want her dead.

"Charles didn't write that," said Agatha. "It doesn't sound like him at all."

"And the word 'marriage' is spelt wrong," added James. "Charles is an educated man. He would never do that."

"I agree," said Bill. "Somehow someone managed to plant this in Charles's email account, but Wilkes is determined to charge him. He's pressing him hard in interviews, waiting for him to slip up."

"Charles has his lawyer there, surely?" Agatha said.

"Of course," Bill assured her. "And he's

cooperating fully, but there is more. From the marks on her neck, the pathologist has come to the conclusion that Mary was strangled by someone with small hands — most likely a woman. Wilkes is out to prove that that woman was you, Agatha. He has a warrant to search your house. They're looking for anything to incriminate you. He and the team will be here in half an hour."

"But I will not," said Agatha, picking up her handbag, car keys and phone and heading for the door. "I have things to do. James, would you stay here and keep an eye on everything for me? Thank you, Bill. I know you're putting your job on the line by being here. You'd best disappear."

Agatha headed for Duns Tew, where she had arranged to meet Toni. She parked her car at the White Horse and walked round to the side road leading to the Lexingtons' house. The sky was heavy with clouds, spreading a premature gloom of dusk, as she approached Toni's car pulling her jacket tight against the slight chill. She settled the pearls at her neck and the stylish decorative pin on her lapel. Toni spotted her coming and wound down her window.

"Seen anything suspicious?" Agatha asked.

"Nothing at all," said Toni, "but there's

no sign of Simon, either."

"Have you tried calling him?"

"No reply. His phone's switched off."

"Wait here and keep trying. I'm going in."

Agatha walked up to the house and rang the doorbell. Jacob Lexington answered.

"You again!" he snapped. "Still snooping around? I thought I told you to stay away from us."

"I came to say how sorry I am for what happened earlier," Agatha explained. "May I come in? I'd like to apologise to Deborah as well."

"Make it quick. We . . . She tires easily."

Agatha was shown into the hall and asked to wait. She glanced into Jacob's den and saw a suitcase lying beside his weights. She was sure that hadn't been there before. Jacob reappeared.

"She will see you now." He waved Agatha into Deborah's room and closed the door behind her.

The room was dimly lit, the last remnants of daylight filtering through the slatted window blinds. Deborah was lying in her hospital bed, covered with a white sheet but wearing a sweatshirt rather than her silk pyjama top.

"Back again?" she said wearily. "What is it this time?"

"Good evening," said Agatha. "I wanted to say how sorry I am that all that business with Mary has been raked over again. It must be awful for you."

She walked towards the bed. The monitors flickered to Deborah's left as before and the paperback, the TV remote and her water sat on the table to her right, along with the bottle of scent. Agatha sniffed the air.

"Such a pretty perfume," she said, picking up the bottle. "And I love the crystal bottle. I've never seen one quite like it. Must be very expensive. There's a nice weight to it." She juggled the bottle from one hand to the other.

"Don't do that," Deborah ordered. "Put it down!"

"Of course," said Agatha. "I would hate to drop it . . ."

She tossed the bottle from her left hand to her right and it slipped through her fingers. Before it had fallen more than a few inches, Deborah's right hand shot out to catch it.

"Nice catch," Agatha congratulated her. "Clumsy of me, but was that just a miracle recovery we witnessed, or does your right arm work perfectly well when you want it to? That might explain why you have your remote control, your water and your treasured perfume — all the things you need most — here on the right. Why would you do that if you couldn't use your right arm to reach them? Why not have the monitors here and your things to your left?"

Deborah flung back the bedsheet and swung her feet slowly down onto the floor. She was wearing jeans and trainers. She reached inside the neck of her sweatshirt, pulled out the cables and dragged them across the bed. They were attached neither to her nor to the monitors.

"If you've worked it all out, then I don't need to pretend with these any more," she said.

"I should have worked it out sooner," Agatha admitted, "but Mary had made so many enemies and you had laid so many false trails to follow. The perfume should have told me pretty much straight away. You waft it around so much that poor Jacob must have walked through a cloud of it when he was dressed up for the masked ball. I smelt it on him when he danced with me."

"The masked ball," Deborah snorted. "What a hoot. Not really for me, though." She stood to face Agatha. "I can walk, even run a bit now, but I've never been much of a dancer."

"You've been building yourself up in secret. The weights in Jacob's den that Toni thought were too light for him were actually being used by you. You've been mobile for some time, yet to the outside world, even to your closest friends, you still appeared to be an invalid."

"Things aren't always what they seem," said Deborah.

"So I keep hearing," Agatha agreed. "The friend who came to see you showed you her invitation to the ball — what did you do? Send her off to make a coffee? She had no idea you could move, no idea when she came back into the room that you had been through her handbag and stolen the invitation."

"That," Deborah admitted, "really was a stroke of luck. We knew the Brown-Fields would have security. It's one of their ways of showing off."

"You knew your way around Barfield House from when you were kids. There are dozens of ways into the main house and Gustav is never entirely conscientious about keeping them all locked, but the Brown-Fields' security people probably would. So you needed someone on the inside. We had Gustav to let us in — we even saw your friend who had lost her invitation causing a scene at the door — and you had Jacob, all dressed up and disguised. I'm assuming he used his computer and design skills to doctor the invitation."

"He's good at that sort of thing." Deborah nodded. "That party came along at just the right time for us. It was too good an opportunity to miss. Once we were in, we just had to coax Mary out of the ballroom. She didn't know Jake. He was going to charm her with some rubbish about horses and tempt her out to the stables. Then you cropped up and made that part easy for us."

"But why dress her in the riding gear?"

"We had to dress her in something. If we were spotted carrying a body, we might have been able to pass her off as a drunk who had passed out, but not when she was naked, straight out of the shower."

"Why move her at all? That was a risky thing to do."

"We know the house. We were pretty confident we could get her down to the stable block without being seen."

"Ah yes, the stables," said Agatha. "That was a big statement from you, wasn't it?"

"I wanted her found there. She did this to me," Deborah pointed to the bed, "and it was all because of her obsession with riding. She was supposed to die there, but you forced her to go upstairs to change."

"What about the faked suicide?" Agatha asked. "You must have known that would have been exposed sooner or later."

"We were hoping for later," said Deborah. "Anything to buy us a bit of time. Maybe people would have seen the suicide as a statement too. She was a failure as a rider, she was a failure as a human being — that sort of thing. Frankly, I was happy for people to read into it whatever they liked, as long as it dragged out the investigation."

"Ah yes, sowing confusion, seeding false leads to cause delays. You knew that Charles would be the prime suspect, naturally, and I take it that Jacob hacked his email account to plant a message apparently sent to a hit man. A false lead. Planting the costume at Tamara's house was another false lead. You had us running around tracking down anyone involved in the show-jumping circuit. You knew that would provide plenty of suspects."

"We were pretty sure Charles would involve you, Mrs. Raisin, and that just served to muddy the waters even further. More delays, more time for us."

"And time is money, isn't it? You sold this house, but when it comes to property, there are a lot of checks and balances to be observed, especially when this much money is involved. There are rules about the transfer of money, rules that ensure the money is going to the right person, rules that make sure there's no fraud involved, that there is no kind of money laundering going on . . . It all takes time, even when the buyer and seller are happy with the deal.

"Even once you got your hands on the money, you couldn't take the chance that it might be frozen in your bank account. That could have happened if you had skipped the country too soon. The suitcase in Jacob's room — you're ready to go, aren't you?"

"We were unlikely suspects, given my condition — or what people thought was my condition. I had plenty of time to lie in a bed thinking of nothing but how to get my own back on that little cow. I came up with dozens of plans for her murder, but no one could know that I was getting better. Me being bed-bound was central to every plan I dreamt up. If I was suddenly to disappear abroad, it would arouse suspicion and that could put our money at risk. It had to go into our regular bank account in the normal way. Then we could safely transfer it out of the country and disappear."

"That's not going to happen now, I'm

afraid." Agatha pointed to the decorative button on her lapel. "Camera. We've got it all recorded. Are you getting all this, Toni?"

The door crashed open.

"Yes, she is," Jacob said, throwing Toni's laptop onto the floor. He flung Toni straight after it. Her wrists were bound in front of her with gaffer tape, and a strip of the stuff covered her mouth. Her feet were not bound, but Jacob had spun her off balance. She groaned as she hit the floor.

"Toni, are you —" Before Agatha could utter another word, Jacob had crossed the room and grabbed her arms, holding them by her sides. His sister quickly looped the monitor cables around her, tying them tight, pinning her arms. Then she pushed her backwards into one of the visitors' chairs.

"Get more tape," she ordered Jacob. "We need to secure this one, too."

"In a second," said Jacob. "Let's have everyone join the party."

He left the room and returned dragging Simon, bound hand and foot with tape and gagged. He dumped him beside Toni, who had propped herself into a sitting position, then stepped back into the hall to retrieve his roll of tape for Agatha.

"You won't get away with this," said Agatha.

"I bet you've said that loads of times, Mrs. Raisin," Deborah sneered, "but this time you're wrong."

Jacob returned with the tape but had taken no more than three steps into the room when Simon launched himself across the floor, rolling like a log and knocking Jacob's legs from under him. Jacob staggered forward and fell to his knees, but he was up again in an instant, turning towards the helpless Simon, who did his best to shuffle away.

"You stupid little piece of shit!" Jacob yelled, landing a kick in Simon's stomach. In the blink of an eye, Toni was on her feet, clutching the laptop in both hands.

"Look out, Jacob!" his sister yelled, but it was too late. Toni brought the laptop crashing down on Jacob's head.

Agatha winced. In the movies, that would have been enough to knock Jacob unconscious, but this wasn't a movie. Agatha knew that in real life when you bashed someone on the head, unless it was with something heavy enough to smash their skull in, all it did was make them angry. It hurt, the shock disorientated them for a second, and then they hit back.

"Run, Toni!" Agatha screamed, but it was too late. Jacob flung out an arm and caught

Toni across the face with the back of his hand. She was knocked to the floor again. Agatha struggled to stand, throwing kicks at Deborah, but then froze when Deborah held the blade of an open pair of scissors to her throat.

"Tape her to the chair, Jake."

Jacob held a hand to his head, then examined the blood on his fingers. He frowned and turned towards Toni.

"This one first," he said. Toni was winded, gasping for breath through the gaffer tape gag. He grabbed her by the wrists, and dragged her towards him in order to reach her ankles and run the roll of tape around them. "Don't want her popping up again all of a sudden."

He then knelt to wind the tape around Agatha's ankles.

"Can't have been much of a life for you, Jacob," said Agatha, "after your sister's accident."

"It was no accident," Deborah corrected her. "That bitch could have killed me."

"All the same," Agatha reasoned, thinking fast and trying to keep a conversation going as long as she could. Now it was her turn to be buying time. "A young man like you, you should have been out there in the big wide world — parties, holidays, girlfriends . . ."

"Tamara has always been besotted with you, hasn't she, Jake?" his sister sniggered.

"Everything might have been different," Jacob said, wrapping tape around Agatha's arms, fixing her to the chair, "if it hadn't been for the Brown-Field girl. She deserved all she got."

"It's not too late for you, you know, Jacob," said Agatha. "Deborah strangled Mary, not you. You could still walk free if you play your cards right."

"We are both walking free, Mrs. Raisin," Jacob replied. "We're heading for a place in the sun. We're leaving all this behind and starting a whole new life. Nothing can stop that now."

"You won't be able to hide forever," said Agatha. "The police will catch up with you eventually."

"Not a chance," Jacob assured her. "New names, new passports, new everything. Jake and Debbie will no longer exist. We've been planning this for a long time, and our flight leaves tonight."

"Unfortunately," added his sister, spreading her hands around Agatha's throat and squeezing gently, "you have given us a few loose ends to tidy up."

"What do we do with them?" asked Jake.

"A fire, I think. We'll burn the place down

with them inside." She released Agatha's neck.

"The new owners," Agatha wheezed, sucking air, "won't be too pleased about that."

"Property developers," Deborah laughed. "They won't care. We'll be doing them a favour. They would only tear the place down anyway. They'll fit four new houses on this site."

"There's a can of petrol in the garage," said Jacob. "I'll —"

Suddenly there was a huge crash, the roar of an engine and the honking of a car horn. Bright lights beamed in through the blinds.

"There goes your garden fence," Agatha said. "Bella has arrived."

The front door flew open and a stream of uniformed officers rushed into the room, filling the air with calls of "Police! Stay where you are! Nobody move!" Then Bill Wong was at her side, cutting the tape and untying the monitor leads.

"Are you all right, Agatha?" he asked.

"Fine," said Agatha, turning to look over her shoulder to where Alice Peterson and another police woman were releasing Toni. Toni nodded to her. A medic was tending to Simon. He saw Agatha looking towards him and gave her one of his wide, wrinkled grins. "They seem fine too. Boy, am I glad to see you, Bill. I was beginning to think you might not make it in time."

"I got the first call from Toni," said Bill, smiling. "We were already on our way when the Colonel demanded reinforcements."

"Agatha, my dear girl!" The Colonel marched into the room carrying his green ledger. "Jen and I were having a damn fine dinner down at the White Horse. Watched it all from there. Boys in blue cut it a bit fine, eh?"

"Colonel, you have been amazing." Agatha went to shake his hand, hesitated, then threw her arms round him. "Thank you so much for all your help."

"Glad to be of service," he said. "Now I must get Bella home. Looks like it's going to rain again. Don't like her out in the rain. Mustn't forget Jen. Left her finishing off an apple and walnut strudel."

"We'll want to talk to you later, Colonel," said Bill, "and Agatha . . ."

"I know," Agatha said, watching Deborah and Jacob being led away in handcuffs. "It's going to be a long night."

CHAPTER TEN

Two days later, Toni and Agatha were driving down the road towards Barfield House, the swish of the tyres on the wet road surface drowning out the noise of the engine. Sunshine flickered through the leaves of overhanging branches, reflecting off the road in patches of glassy glare. The heatwave had broken with a series of heavy rain showers and the Cotswold spring was now settling into its more usual gentle, milder weather.

Following a harrowing Monday night of questions, form-filling and more questions, Agatha had given her entire team the day off on Tuesday, with her secretary left holding the fort in the office. Mrs. Freedman had let the phone ring off the hook and spent most of the day drinking tea, reading a rather raunchy bodice-ripper lent to her by Agatha and shouting, "No comment!" down the stairs when reporters rattled the letter box, just as Agatha had instructed. Today they were all back at work, and now that the file marked "Fraith Murder Inquiry" was complete and nestling safely in Agatha's briefcase, things were beginning to get back to normal. There were more missing pets, more employers with security concerns . . . and lots more divorces. Murder, Agatha decided, was actually quite good for business, unless, of course, you were the victim, in which case you could consider yourself liquidated.

Roy Silver had set off for London early that morning, but his new-found passion for riding now made him more likely than ever to become a regular weekend visitor. He was happy to carry on working with Tamara and had been a huge comfort to her when he broke the news about Jacob. The police, of course, had visited the stables, evidence was collected and Tamara had been interviewed at length, but the press were now portraying her as a victim of both "Bloody Mary" — every journalist loved that term — and "the Lexington Stranglers," "the Sinister Siblings" and "the Evil Twins." The Lexingtons were not twins, but the news editor who had come up with the tag wasn't about to let that fact get in the way of a good headline.

Roy was milking the media attention for all it was worth and had been forced back to his London office to deal with the surge of interest in the Montgomery Stables from corporate clients and equestrian sponsors. Tamara had shut reporters out of the stables, upset by events and unable to cope with their pestering. She kept her head down and pointed everyone towards Roy. Agatha knew that she would cope well enough once things settled down and people wanted to talk to her about horses and riding instead of intrigue and murder. That would come soon enough. The press had little interest in yesterday's news.

"Are you sure you want me to drop you off at the bottom of the drive?" said Toni. "I can come in with you if you like."

"I'm sure," said Agatha. "It's so refreshing outside. The rain has stopped and it's a beautiful day for a walk in the fresh air."

"It's just . . . you're going in on your own."

"I'll be fine. We don't have to do everything mob-handed. And you need to take yourself off shopping. That dress you were wearing on Monday evening was ruined after you were flung around the room and dragged across the floor. Get yourself a new one. Get a couple — charge them to the company. I've got Charles's invoice in here."

She patted the briefcase on her lap. "Raisin Investigations can afford it."

Toni turned into the gateway to Barfield House and Agatha hopped out of the car. She set off up the long avenue of trees with a spring in her step. It was indeed a splendid afternoon for a walk. She carried her briefcase in one hand and a bottle-shaped padded bag in the other. In the bag was a chilled bottle of champagne, with which she and Charles would celebrate the successful outcome of the case and his new-found wealth.

As she approached the house, she spotted a small open-topped sports car parked near the terrace and saw some movement on the terrace itself, near the library doors. She carried on walking and recognised the unmistakably neat, slim outline of Sir Charles Fraith — but who was that with him? Venturing a little farther, she could see a young woman, wearing a midnight-blue evening gown that trailed on the ground. The high-heeled shoes that would lift her to the level where the dress simply caressed the ground were in her left hand. Her right hand was stroking Charles's hair, then at the back of his neck as they pressed close to one another and he crushed her to his chest, their lips locked in a kiss that betrayed a lingering lust from the night before. And probably the morning after, too, Agatha guessed, knowing Charles. A long, lazy morning, a very late lunch . . . She felt a chill run down her spine. Had it really taken him so little time to slip back into his old predatory ways?

She watched the young woman wave cheerfully to Charles, throw her shoes into the car's passenger footwell and then climb behind the wheel. Clever girl. You're not used to those new shoes, are you? They must have been hell last night, and your feet still too raw to wear them today. Better to go without them, especially if you're unaccustomed to driving in such high heels.

Charles walked back into the library. Agatha stepped off the drive behind a tree and dropped her briefcase. She took the champagne out of the cooler bag, ripped off the foil and undid the wire. The sports car's engine burst into life and it came zipping down the driveway. Agatha stepped out from the tree, vigorously shaking the champagne. The cork shot out and she crammed her thumb over the mouth of the bottle just as the car reached her, the spray of champagne drenching the driver. The car screeched to a halt and the spray subsided.

"Sorry!" Agatha called, picking up her

briefcase and carrying on up the drive with the bottle held high. "Must have jiggled it!"

Charles was taking a phone call when she walked in through the library's French doors.

"Aggie," he said, hanging up and frowning. "Just had a call from a friend of mine. Warned me there's a madwoman on the drive spraying champagne everywhere."

"I had a bit of an accident," Agatha admitted, setting the bottle on Charles's desk. "I must have jiggled it. It could have been worse, though. They say that one bottle in every few thousand has a flaw in the glass and explodes completely. A friend, was she?"

"Yes . . . a friend."

"Known her long? Probably not, I'd say. She didn't look old enough for anyone to have known her for very long."

"I . . . um . . . met her last night at a Young Farmers' dinner. I was giving a speech about . . . Oh, what the hell, Aggie — I don't have to explain myself to you."

"No, no you don't. Of course you don't. But I was far too knackered to do anything except sleep last night, having spent all my waking hours recently fighting to keep you out of jail!"

"Calm down, for goodness' sake. Let's get this business settled now. The sooner it's all done and dusted, the better."

"Then I'd better update you on what's in the report," Agatha informed him, and gave him a brief account of everything that had happened since they last spoke, including her adventure in France with the beautiful Claudette.

Charles reached for the little handbell on his desk and tinkled it. "GUSTAV!"

Gustav duly appeared and scowled at Agatha.

"I used the tradesmen's entrance," she said. "Like the hired help is supposed to."

"Apparently there has been some kind of Champagne incident on the drive," said Gustav.

Charles waved a hand in the direction of Agatha and the near-empty bottle. "She says she 'jiggled it,' " he said. "Show the gentlemen in, please, Gustav."

"Gentlemen?" queried Gustav. "Will these two do instead?"

He waved Chief Inspector Wilkes and Darell Brown-Field into the room.

"Well, well," said Agatha. "Pinky and Perky. You've just cut the room's average IQ in half."

"I am not here to be insulted by you, Agatha Raisin," muttered Wilkes.

"No?" said Agatha. "What exactly *are* they

288

here for, Charles?"

"I think this one is here to apologise," said Charles, pointing at Wilkes, "and this one," he indicated Brown-Field, "is here to take a last look."

"I don't owe anyone an apology," Wilkes hissed. "I was just doing my job."

"Really?" said Agatha. "If you had done your job properly, the murderers would not have come within an ace of jetting off to a sun-kissed shore somewhere, never to be seen again."

"We were pursuing all valid lines of inquiry!" he insisted.

"You were pursuing me and Charles!" Agatha yelled. "For personal reasons and . . ." she turned to Brown-Field, "perhaps personal gain. Wilkes is one of your golfing chums, isn't he, Darell? You were pressing him to go after Charles and me, weren't you?"

"That Lexington pair have yet to stand trial," blustered Darell. "Who's to say they did this all on their own? Who's to say *he* isn't behind it all?"

"The Lexingtons themselves, Darell," said Agatha. "They confessed to everything. We got it all on camera."

"That means nothing!" Darell argued. "They are likely being well paid to carry the can for this. They're young. They'll spend a few years in prison and then they'll be free. They can go and live on a tropical island, or whatever they were planning to do, in comfort for the rest of their lives with a fat load of cash."

"It all comes down to money with you, doesn't it, Darell?" said Agatha. "If Charles had been guilty, his whole estate would be yours. Because he's innocent, you lose all of this," she waved a hand around the room, "and a huge chunk of the Brown-Field millions as well. That's why you had your little lapdog here go after him."

"I am nobody's little —"

"Down, boy," said Agatha, wagging a finger at Wilkes. "Shall we all take a seat, Charles, or is he not allowed on the furniture?"

"I refuse to be treated like this!" shouted Wilkes. "Mircester Police have already issued an official apology. What more do you want from me?"

"How about a bit of a grovel?" Agatha suggested. "You have made life so uncomfortable for Charles and for me; maybe you should consider grovelling a little, otherwise I might feel obliged to start looking into your affairs, the way I did with him!" She nodded towards Darell.

"I warned you to keep your nose out!" Darell yelled, stepping towards her, a clenched fist raised.

"Don't even think about it!" warned Charles, grabbing Darell by the shoulder and pushing him back.

"No, Darell," said Agatha, "don't even think about it. Not in front of witnesses. Not in front of an officer of the law. You are in plain sight, here, not skulking out of a taxi to meet your mistress at a rented house in Oxford."

"I . . . I don't know what you're talking about," Darell blustered.

"Oh but you do, Darell," said Agatha. "Mrs. Sheraton Chadwick is what we're talking about." She reached into her brief-case and pulled out a print of the photograph she'd taken at the restaurant in the Gironde. "You remember her — you were screwing her in France a few days ago. By now the lovely Sherry will be starting to find her whole world falling apart. Her husband has been provided with a preliminary report on her activities here, in France, and with her lovers in Italy, Germany and the Netherlands. Did you know about them? No? Really, Darell — did you think you were her one and only?

"I'm guessing you first met her after Mary

tried to nobble her horse. You would have offered her money to hush it all up. Sherry likes money. I wonder what Mrs. Brown-Field will think of all this? I may still be able to keep your name out of the Chadwick divorce. Maybe we can do a deal, Darell. You like doing deals, don't you?"

"What sort of a deal?" muttered Darell.

"How about you leave here, you leave Charles alone and you leave Tamara Montgomery alone, and I will keep you anonymous in the final report."

"That sounds like blackmail," said Wilkes.

"Stay out of this, Wilkes," ordered Darell, "if you want to keep your job long enough to see your pension."

"That sounds like very good advice," said Charles. "Best keep your trap shut, old boy."

"So what about it, Darell?" Agatha asked. "It would be a bit of a blow to lose Mary's share of your fortune to Charles in a marriage settlement, and then have your wife walk off with the lion's share of the rest in a divorce settlement. Would you be left with enough to interest little Sherry? Would you still be able to afford gifts like the horse brooch you had made for her? Did she see the one Mary had and demand one the same?"

"You gave your *whore* a brooch like

Mary's!" Linda Brown-Field was standing in the library doorway. She strutted towards Darell and slapped him across the face. "You gave *her* a copy of the gift *I* had made for *my* daughter! How could you?"

"Linda, darling, I only —"

"Shut up!" She slapped him again. Agatha was enjoying this. "You've got a lot to answer for. From now on, we'll be doing things *my* way."

She turned to Charles.

"We are leaving this house. You will not see or hear from us again. We will retire to Marbella."

She looked at Agatha.

"Tamara Montgomery will not hear from us again either, but you may, Mrs. Raisin, should I ever have need of your services. Did you hear that, Darell, you shitty little cockroach?"

She glared at Wilkes.

"And if you ever show your face at my house in Marbella again, you pathetic old arse-licker, I will set *her* on you!"

She turned and marched out.

"I think now would be a good time for you two to leave," said Charles, addressing Darell and Wilkes. He tinkled the little bell. "GUSTAV!"

Gustav walked into the room and sighed.

"Has it ever occurred to you," he said, "that ringing the bell is rendered redundant when you follow it up by bawling like a Mircester market trader?"

"See the chief inspector out, Gustav," said Charles. "Then help Mr. Brown-Field pack. Make sure he doesn't purloin any of the family silver."

"You sold that years ago," muttered Gustav, ushering the wearied Wilkes and the forlorn Darell out of the room.

"I must be going too," said Agatha, taking a folder from her briefcase. "Here is your report, and here is my invoice for payment."

"Here is your cheque," said Charles.

"You haven't looked at the invoice."

"I don't need to. This will more than cover it — plus a bonus."

"Very generous. I think my team have earned it."

"Aggie, must we be like this?" Charles pleaded, reaching out to touch her. "Can't we go back to the way it used to be with us?"

Agatha backed away. "There's not going to be any 'us,' Charles. Certainly not after you came home from the Young Farmers' dinner with the prize cow."

"Don't be like that."

"I've done my job. I've done what you

paid me for. I was hired to help. Now I'm going."

She walked out onto the terrace, turned right towards the driveway, realised that she had no car and marched back past Charles, down onto the lawn and off towards the woods. The Huntsman would be open. She would have a drink and call for a taxi.

Charles watched Agatha's departure with a mixture of regret and irritation. She had stormed out of Barfield countless times in the past, but she'd never headed into the woods before. That had to mean something. Maybe this time she was going for good. He wandered back into the library and sat down behind his desk, pondering all that had happened.

"GUSTAV!"

"What, no bell?"

"Book me on the next available flight to Bordeaux. There's a young lady there I think I should meet."

Agatha's taxi did not arrive outside the Huntsman until she had tucked away three deceptively large glasses of Pinot Gris, which wasn't really surprising as she hadn't called for it until she was halfway through her second. The pub was quiet and the barmaid was more than willing to chat about wine, men, shoes, men, clothes, men, cats and men. Only wine, shoes, clothes and cats came out well from their conversation.

James was tidying his front garden when the taxi pulled up in Lilac Lane. Agatha exited the car a little unsteadily and paused, fumbling for her door keys.

"James!" she announced, swaying slightly. "You are a good man, but tomorrow I am going back to France, where they have wine . . ." she surprised herself with a burp, "where they have fashion, grapes and fruity men. It's what life's all about . . . and cats."

She disappeared into her cottage. James considered following her to make sure she was all right, but sensibly decided against it. If he heard any crashes, screams or other signs of distress, he would reconsider. He did not, and when he later ventured a peek through Agatha's front window, he saw her curled up sound asleep on the sofa. All things considered, he thought, that was the best place for her. If she really was off to France again tomorrow, he would feed her cats. He was pretty sure that was what she had meant.

Agatha rolled off the sofa well before dawn and dragged herself upstairs to the shower. By the time the weak early-morning sun crept over the hills to tinge the tired night clouds a rejuvenating pink, she was on her way to Moreton-in-Marsh to catch a London-bound train. The train, at first almost empty, became ever more crowded with the wave of morning commuters surging towards the capital. Arriving at Paddington station, she took the Underground to St. Pancras, where she boarded the Eurostar direct to Paris Gare du Nord, catching a brief nap as the train sped through the tunnel beneath the English Channel. In Paris, a swift Métro ride brought her to Gare Montparnasse, where she took a train for Bordeaux and relaxed with a late lunch and a brave but restorative glass of Sauvignon Blanc before studying a map she had bought to plan her route out of the city.

It was late afternoon by the time the train pulled in to Bordeaux Saint-Jean station. Agatha slung her modest overnight bag into a rental car and drove down to the river, following the Garonne until the swirling glass-and-steel tower of the Cité du Vin museum loomed into sight. There she turned left and slowed frustratingly in a snarl of sluggish traffic crawling along a boulevard that passed an old dockyard to the right from where Italian submarines had set sail during the Second World War to join the German U-boat wolf packs attacking convoys in the Atlantic. That was yet another fact that James had slipped into their conversation when he had first heard she was visiting Bordeaux. She congratulated herself on having remembered.

She turned right onto the Boulevard Aliénor d'Aquitaine, named after the woman who had been Queen of France, Queen of England and the most powerful woman in Europe during the twelfth century. She really was surprising herself with how much of James's waffle she had managed to soak up while only half listening. She could probably learn a lot if she actually paid attention. Her route then took her onto a bridge across a city lake before she picked up a road that led out through the suburbs into the Gironde countryside.

She emerged from the vineyard at the chateau and immediately saw Claudette skipping down the staircase to greet her.

"Agatha!" Claudette squealed, throwing her arms around her and kissing her on both cheeks. "I am so happy that you are here again!"

"I'm very pleased to be here. How is Pascal?"

"He is very well and looking forward to seeing you this evening. He is out touring the vineyard with a friend. Now come inside, I think it may be starting to rain."

They hurried inside and Claudette organised tea for them in the drawing room. They settled into chairs with a view through the tall windows over the vineyards that stretched off to the far horizon. The first spots of light rain peppered the glass.

"It is so nice to be back," said Agatha, "but there is something I must talk to you about, Claudette."

"You sound so serious. What is it that is troubling you?"

"Do you know anything about CPD Developments?"

"Why do you ask?"

"CPD Developments is part of CPD Holdings, an investment company. CPD is Claudette-Pascal-Duvivier, isn't it? Both companies are owned by you and your uncle."

"That is correct," said Claudette, sounding a little defensive. "We have many companies involved in property investments."

"You must be aware that CPD Developments bought Deborah and Jacob Lexington's house for a vastly inflated sum."

"They needed money." Claudette shrugged. "I felt sorry for them. They had been through so much. My uncle and I decided to help them. I know what it is like to lose your parents so young, and then there was the incident with Mary Brown-Field . . ."

"Did you know that Deborah was able to walk again?"

"I visited them once or twice. I could see that she was getting better."

"I wouldn't have thought of the two of you as friends."

"How is it that you say in English . . . the enemy of my enemy is my friend!"

"I thought your fight with Mary was just a storm in a teacup, so to speak."

"You do not know it all. No one except Uncle Pascal and Pierre knows. No one saw. I caught her in our transporter with the horses. What I told you about her trying to kick me and me hitting her with my hat was true, but then . . ."

Claudette lifted her T-shirt to show Agatha a livid scar running diagonally across her abdomen from just below her left breast to just above her right hip. Agatha caught her breath.

"She did that?"

"She took a steel bale hook — we use for lifting hay bales — from a wall rack and swipe me. I was lucky. It is not too deep, no major damage, but when it happen, there was a lot of blood. I was in much pain and collapsed. I could not move. She did not call for help. She took a rag, wiped clean the bale hook of her fingerprints, then left. Pierre found me.

"I could not compete, could not ride for months. Now I am well again, but this," she ran a finger down the scar, then smoothed her T-shirt back into place, "this is for keeps, and not so good in bikini weather, no?"

"You could have had her thrown in jail."

"With no witnesses, I think not. We say it was an accident and I look for a way to pay her back."

"So you paid the Lexingtons to kill her?"

"Kill?" Claudette shrugged again. "How do I know they would do that? We make sure they have enough money to move abroad, start a new life, that is all."

"How did that help you to pay Mary back?"

"Every little bit helps . . ."

"I'm afraid I don't believe you, Claudette," said Agatha, standing, "but I doubt I will ever be able to prove that you were involved in the murder plan. I'm not entirely sure that I even want to try, but I don't think I can stay here either. I'm going to head back to Carsely. I will see myself out."

"I am sorry you feel this way, but of

course you must do as you wish. *Au revoir,* Agatha."

"No," said Agatha. "*Adieu,* Claudette."

Agatha had made it as far as one of the sweeping staircases outside the front door when she saw two figures walking up the other side. Two men. She knew both of them. One was Pascal, the other was Sir Charles Fraith. She turned and took up position at the top of their staircase.

"Aggie!" called Charles, beaming a smile up at her. "What a fantastic surprise. How lovely to see you —"

"YOU!" shrieked Agatha, jabbing a finger at him. "What the hell are you doing here?"

"He has come to research the vines," explained Pascal, "perhaps make English wine and —"

"A likely story!" Agatha snapped. "You have no interest in vines. You might, of course, have an interest in Claudette!"

"Well, naturally, Claudette and I —"

"How long have you been seeing her? Wait a minute . . . you were in on it, weren't you?" Agatha roared, taking a neatly logical step to entirely the wrong conclusion. "You were in on the murder right from the beginning — with them, and with the Lexingtons! You have played me for a fool all along!"

"Aggie, sweetie, I —"

"Don't call me that!" she shrieked. "Don't say another word! I never want to see you again! Stay away from me! Stay out of my life! You hear me? STAY OUT OF MY LIFE!"

She ran down the stairs, leapt into the hire car and sped off along the road through the vineyard.

"What . . . what was all that about, Pascal?" gasped Charles.

"I have no idea." Pascal shrugged, casting a furtive glance at Agatha's departing car.

"But she mentioned the murder, and the Lexingtons. You don't know the Lexingtons, do you?"

"I know no one of that name," Pascal lied.

"She was so upset . . ."

"I think it is what women do best," said Pascal, taking Charles gently by the arm. "Perhaps she has been working too hard. Too much stress. Too much murder on her mind. Now come, let us try some of our wine . . ."

Agatha caught an early-evening train from Bordeaux to Paris. She considered finding a hotel room to break her journey, go for a stroll and find somewhere nice for dinner. The idea was short-lived. She loved the sounds, the smells and the feel of Paris. It was such a romantic city . . . and that was her problem. She was on her own. Had she been able to share an evening in the City of Light, walking along the banks of the Seine, even in the drizzly rain that was now falling, would have been a huge pleasure. On her own, it was a damp, miserable prospect.

Studying her timetables, she worked out that she could make it to Paddington for the late train back to Moreton. Instead of a romantic dinner in the French capital, she would grab a sandwich from the Eurostar buffet on the way to London.

It was almost one o'clock in the morning by the time she reached Carsely and parked her car in Lilac Lane. Her cottage was in darkness. There was a light on in James's dining room. Agatha knew that he often worked late, finding it easier to write when most of the rest of the village was sound asleep and there were no other distractions. She climbed out of her car and the click of the door closing brought him to his study window. She walked up his path rather than hers, knowing that he would come to the door.

"What's happened?" he asked, keeping his

voice low. "Aren't you supposed to be in a chateau somewhere in France?"

"I am, or I was, but . . . I just wanted to come home, James."

"I see," said James, hearing exhaustion and despair in her voice. "French men not fruity enough?"

"What?"

"Never mind," he said, smiling. "You look dead beat. That's quite a round trip you've had."

"I know, and . . . Oh James, I feel like such a fool . . . a complete idiot . . ."

"You're not," he said, putting his arms around her. "You're just tired. The whole murder thing has worn you out."

She looked up at him and he kissed her gently.

"Don't be on your own tonight," he whispered. "Stay with me." He held his arms up in mock surrender. "No rumpy-pumpy, I promise. Just stay with me."

She hugged him tight. "I would love that," she said. They went inside together and the light in the study window clicked off.

ABOUT THE AUTHOR

M. C. Beaton (1936–2019), the "Queen of Crime" (*The Globe and Mail*), was the author of the *New York Times* and *USA Today* bestselling Agatha Raisin novels — the basis for the hit show on Acorn TV and public television — as well as the Hamish Macbeth series and the Edwardian Murder Mysteries featuring Lady Rose Summer. Born in Scotland, she started her career writing historical romances under several pseudonyms and her maiden name, Marion Chesney.